T0357179

WHEN
WE
RiDE

Also by Rex Ogle

Free Lunch

Punching Bag

Abuela, Don't Forget Me

Road Home

WHEN WE RiDE

A NOVEL

REX OGLE

NORTON YOUNG READERS
An Imprint of W. W. Norton & Company
Independent Publishers Since 1923

For information about permission to reproduce selections from this book, write to
Permissions, W. W. Norton & Company, Inc., 500 Fifth Avenue, New York, NY 10110

For information about special discounts for bulk purchases, please contact
W. W. Norton Special Sales at specialsales@wwnorton.com or 800-233-4830

Manufacturing by Lakeside Book Company
Book design by Hana Anouk Nakamura
Production manager: Delaney Adams

ISBN 978-1-324-05282-1

W. W. Norton & Company, Inc., 500 Fifth Avenue, New York, NY 10110
www.wwnorton.com

W. W. Norton & Company Ltd., 15 Carlisle Street, London W1D 3BS

10 9 8 7 6 5 4 3 2 1

For Marshall.

I miss driving around with you.

i'm waiting to die
the second
they kick in the door
—the drug dealer
and his crew—
'cause I know
it's gonna be bad
'cause their
guns
are already out.

I'm shoved up against the wall,
punched in the stomach
so hard
I
      can't
            breathe.

A tattooed forearm
crushes my throat,
choking me.
Then
the gun
      the gun
          the *GUN*
pinches my temple,
metal pressing into skin
as I stare cross-eyed
at the finger on the trigger,
waiting
for my brains to smear the wall
like red paint . . .

That's when
Lawson's dealer
starts screaming,
"WHERE'S MY MONEY?!"

you know how they say

when you're about to die
your life flashes
before your eyes?

Yeah,
that's what I'm about to do.

SEPTEMBER

i'm driving
my best friend
around town
'cause that's what friends do.

Take care of each other.
Have each other's backs
even when the world
                         doesn't.

weed

Pot.
Bud.
Mary Jane.
Ganja.
Herb.
Grass.
Chronic.
Dope.
Hash.
Trees.
Hemp.
Cannabis.
Marijuana.

Folks like to smoke them
Bongs.
Blunts.
Doobies.
Phatties.
Spliffs.
Wood pipes.
Metal pipes.
Ceramic pipes.
Glass pipes.
Even outta apples.
And of course,
joints,
        all the way down to the tail end
                        they call a roach.

I'm not judging.
I don't smoke though.
That shit makes you stupid.
And I can't afford to be stupid.
I'm dumb enough as it is.

But my best friend, Lawson, he smokes.

He sells too.

his pass off

is real quick
'cause Lawson is real slick.
At school, he's walking the hall,
blond hair, blue eyes, six feet tall,
in a big puffer jacket,
gold chains around white neck,
and gives a nod
to someone else who gives a nod,
then they lean in,
shoulder to shoulder,
shake hands.
Only they're not shaking,
they're exchanging.

Lawson's a magician,
only instead of making coins or cards
appear from nowhere,
his fingers transform
green bagged bud
into
green cash money.

He's too fast,
like a basketball flashing past.
Teachers don't see it.
Students don't see it.

But I see it.

But I don't say nothin'
to nobody.

"you gotta get in on this,"

Lawson says,
over the cafeteria buzz
of students talking and eating.
"Dime bags be selling like hotcakes."
I ask, "*Who's selling hotcakes for ten bucks a pop?*"
Lawson counts his money just under the table,
saying, "Ten, twenty, thirty, forty, fifty,"
green paper flashing against pink fingers,
Lawson looking my way, smiling bright white teeth,
"Selling weed is easy money."

"*Nah, I'm good,*"
I say, looking at my own Mexican brown skin,
kissed browner by the summer sun,
as I study while I eat.
"*I got a job.*"

"Busing tables ain't a real job.
Busing tables ain't gonna get you no girlfriend.
Busing tables ain't gonna put you through college neither.
Plus,
that shit
don't pay shit."

I don't say it,
but he's right
especially
about that last part.

after school

I go to work.

I hate this job
working a diner,
at seventeen years old,
busing tables,
hoping this job is
temporary,
and not my fate.

I hate this job
having to wear an apron and a stupid hat,
picking up plates of half-eaten sausage
yellow egg scraps
(two-dollar) silver dollar pancakes
slathered with sticky syrup that sticks to my fingers
as it all goes into a black bus tub
along with mugs
of undrunk coffee refills
and half-used plastic bullets
of creamer.

I hate this job
but one can't be picky
in a college town
where jobs are few and far between.

I hate this job
even more
when kids from my high school
come in
and laugh in my direction.

i almost forgot

to introduce myself.
(My bad.)

My dad named me
Diego Miguel Benevides
when I was born
but always called me
"Deegs"
          . . . before he left.

Mom calls me
"Diego"
except when she's mad,
growling
"Diego Miguel, I swear to God . . ."

But Lawson Pierce,
when we were eight years young,
he dubbed me
"Benny."

I asked,
"Why you keep calling me Benny?"

He said,
"'Cause Diego Miguel Bene-whatever has too many
whatcha call 'em . . .
syllables.
'S too much work to say the whole thing.
Benny's easier."

then one day

when we were nine,
instead of calling me Benny,
Lawson said,
"Yo, brother. What's good?"

With no siblings,
I've always been an only child,
just like Lawson.

"I'm not your brother."

"Yeah you are,"
he said.
"Brothers ain't always made by blood.
Sometimes?
Sometimes,
brothers just find each other."

lawson and i

met in third grade,
when he moved into the place
across the street
from my place
and waved.
I was too shy to wave back.

But at school
at recess
this older kid, Donnie, closed in on me, said,
"Heard your dad took off. Probably 'cause he hated your face.
Know what? So do I."
He shoved me so hard, I fell,
scraping hands and knees,
fresh blooms of red
running down my legs
like ribbons
into my socks.

Lawson walked up,
said, "My dad left too. Ain't your fault. Dads suck."
He offered his hand,
helped me up . . .

. . . then punched Donnie in the face.

Lawson and me,
we've been best friends
ever since.

We used to play at the playground,
swinging on swings,
to see who could get highest
before jumping off
to land in the sand
without falling over
like Olympic gymnasts.

We used to swim at the public pool,
leaping off the high dive,
making faces underwater,
seeing who could hold their breath longest,
before buying chocolate
from the snack bar
that would melt
under the August sun
all over
our young hands.

We used to sneak into his freezer
stealing from the box of Toaster Strudels,
clear packets of white cream frosting
which we would suck down greedily
like mosquitoes
needing sugar
'til his mom would catch us,
chase us outta the kitchen,
her fly swatter swatting at our legs.

We used to play G.I. Joe
with our four-inch-tall action figures
camouflaged in green and brown army gear
bearing small plastic knives and rifles and guns
when we thought guns were cool
before we saw the remains
of a drive-by shooting
down the street.

That was before . . .
before high school,
before Lawson grew tall,
before he started failing classes,
before he got kicked off the basketball team,
before he started
          selling.

But we never stopped hanging out.
We never stopped being brothers
from different mothers.

Now
we're high school seniors
trying to figure out our futures . . .

    . . . if we ever get that far.

our neighborhood

used to be nice
like thirty years ago
according to my mom.

Now,
trash in the street.
Trash on people's lawns
growing wild with weeds.
Cars on bricks in front yards.
Angry pit bulls barking mad.
Paint flaking off houses like dry skin.
Bars on windows, like detention centers.
Junkies walking up the asphalt, day and night,
dressed in layers of dirtied rags, barefoot,
with sleeping bags over shoulders
like fur coats,
not bothering to hide
black and blue bruises
of track marks on their arms
as they wander streets, yards, sidewalks,
searching sleepy-eyed
for their next fix.

The rest of us try to get by,
working
or trying to find work
to buy food, pay bills, and rent an old house
that's falling apart.
Mom says she's lucky,
working two jobs,
housekeeping hotels and housekeeping homes
six days a week,
taking off only on Sundays for church,
then after, volunteering,
taking care of old people
even though she's tired
and someone
should be taking care
of her.

I say, "*Let me help. What can I do?*"
"Stay out of trouble. Stay in school. Study. Graduate. Go to college.
You can help me

by helping yourself."

my mom

doesn't know
when I was little
I thought she was a saint
'cause she looked like Our Lady of Guadalupe
whose image was all over the church
and on one of Dad's candles
in the bathroom.
Both women have
dark hair
light skin
and a solemn smile
as if they have a secret
others don't know.

Mom met Dad in high school
made me too early
so their parents
forced them to get married
before they were ready.

When I was eight,
I won a coloring contest
at the grocery store,
got twenty-five bucks.
Mom said,
"Let's open a savings account
for you
for college."

She's always saying,
"Education is everything.
And you're going to college
if it's the last thing I do."

Mom didn't go to college
which is why
she wants me to go so bad.

I say,
"*I'm not gonna get in.*"
She says,
"You won't know if you don't apply."
"*We don't have money for application fees.*"
"I've been saving up."
"*We don't have money to pay for college.*"
"You'll get scholarships."
"*And if not?*"
"You will."
"*And if not?*"
"In-state universities are very affordable."
"*We can't afford those either.*"
"Then you can take out loans."
"*No one in our family's ever gone to college.*"
"Then you'll be the first."
"*Mom, I'm trying to be real with you.
Chances are low,
like slim to none.
I'm nobody.*"

"Everyone has to start somewhere,"
she says.
"You're smart.
You work hard.
You'll get in."

I wanna believe her.

But I don't know if I do.

just in case
I fill out the applications

I write the essays

and send them in

        dreaming

           of tomorrows

              better than today.

lawson says,
"I need a ride."

He always needs a ride.

I don't mind 'cause

I've never had a brother,
but if I did
I'd want him to be
just like Lawson.

He's my ride-or-die

. . . though . . .

preferably
            without
                    the dying.

plus

Lawson always pays for gas.

He pays with
two crisp ten-dollar bills,
or four worn, tired fives,
or twenty faded and wrinkled ones
found in his pocket.

The same
tens and fives and ones
he earns
selling weed.

I try not to mind.

It's just weed . . .

right?

my car is old school

1980 Cadillac DeVille,
silver outside,
red leather inside,
tape deck that plays
old cassette tapes I buy
at Goodwill for fifty cents a pop.

The car's metal body
drives like a tank.
To turn,
I turn the steering wheel
around and around and around again,
like one of those big boats on TV.

The A/C doesn't work
so I drive windows down.
I like the fresh air anyway.

Mom
drove this car
for two decades,
before she gave me the keys,
saying, "You need this, to drive to work and school and the library."
I asked, "*How are you gonna get around?*"
"That's what the bus is for."
"*Mom, you can't—*"
"I can. And I will. You are everything.
And I want you to succeed."
Mom says, "She's not new, but she drives.
Her name is María Carmen."

"*You named the car?*"

"Of course. If you treat her well,
she'll treat you well."

So I buy a rabbit's foot
for luck
to hang from the rearview,

and say, petting her dashboard,
"*Please don't break on me, María Carmen.*
I need a car."

one hand out the window
trying to catch the wind
my other hand
on the steering wheel.
Breeze rolls in
tossing my hair
this way and that.

Lawson turns up the radio
belting out
"Out on bail fresh outta jail, California dreamin'
Soon as I stepped on the scene, I'm hearin' hoochies screamin',"
knowing every word by heart
of 2Pac's "California Love"
while I know
just the chorus
and the music video
set in a Mad Max future.

"Go faster," Lawson says.
I shake my head,
"*No*,"
'cause I know better
than to drive too fast
with cops in this town
looking for any reason
to pull
my
Mexican
ass
over

and give me trouble.

outside the 7-eleven

Lawson waits
on one foot,
the other planted on the bricks of the wall
he leans against.

A man comes out,
hands a paper bag
to Lawson,
who hands the stranger money
in return.

Lawson always makes sure
to get his first,
before giving up anything.

"Score," he says,
hopping in my car,
glass-bottled beer in the brown bag.
"I got my forty."
Lawson's drink of choice?
Four-zero ounces of
Olde English malt liquor.

He says,
"Let's party."

friday night

I park María Carmen outside a rager.
Lawson leads the way,
me following,
up the sidewalk
into a house
ten times the size
of the rental Mom and I
squeeze into.

The rooms are overflowing
with talking
with laughter
with shouting over music
from teenagers I know
and teenagers I don't,
all of them, red plastic Solo cup in hand,
getting messed up for the weekend's sake.

I put ice in a cup,
fill it with ginger ale
so if anyone asks,
I can save face
while I lie
saying:
"*I'm drinking vodka soda.*"

You're probably wondering why I don't drink.
My mom's trying to stay sober.
I wanna set a good example.

But don't tell her I said that.

sitting on the couch
is where I always end up at parties.
I don't mind.
I like to watch
people moving around
talking,
dancing,
drinking,
smoking weed
      from aluminum cans
           or carved-out apples.

Lawson moves about
like a butterfly,
whispering in ears,
doing his wizard thing,
shaking hands,
transforming
bud into cash.

Everyone is having all the fun
           except for me.

Then someone spills a beer on me
           and now I'm wet.

my mom

used to come home
six-pack tucked under arm
slurring words
wobbling on feet
shouting at Dad
'til shouts became screams.

When she passed out,
Dad'd be cleaning up puke
all down her chin and the couch
onto the floor, littered
with brown bottles and aluminum cans
and roaches,
       so many roaches,
             both buds and bugs.

It took six years,
but Dad left her

             and me.

After she got sober,
Mom made me swear,
"Promise me,
       you won't be like me."

       And I promised.

That's probably why
I am the way I am
always trying to be
            in control.

That means,
no smoking,
no drinking,
no fucking around.

I don't wanna be
like my mom used to be.
I gotta be
                    better.

people get loose

on the dance floor
which is really just the living room
with a coffee table pushed to the wall.
Bodies grinding against bodies
red cups raised to the sky
in prayer
to thank the party gods.

I can't dance
so I watch from the couch
like a plush cushion
'til Lawson grabs me
hauls me
onto my feet
and over the vibrating music
shouts in my ear
"Benny,
live a little,"
and pushes me into a girl.

He's always doing stuff like that.

Making me do stuff I don't wanna,
that ends up being kinda fun anyway.

That's part of why I like him.
Why I wanna be like him.
'Cause he's alive
in ways I wanna be
but don't know how.

"hangovers are the worst,"

Lawson says,
the next morning
holding his heavy, aching head.

"I wouldn't know."

"Still tricking that trick,
pouring Sprite into your Solo cup,
saying it's vodka soda?"

"Ginger ale. But yeah."

"Smart boy."

OCTOBER

in the park

we sit on a bench.
I do my homework,
while Lawson smokes menthol cigarettes.

He flicks ashes,
then flicks the pages of my textbook.
"Why you bother with that shit?
Grades don't mean nothin' in the real world.
They're just letters and numbers."

"Letters and numbers now
turn into jobs later."

"Fuck later,"
Lawson says.
"All we got is now."

in the park

we sit on a bench.
I do my homework,
while Lawson sells weed
to seniors who go to our school,

while Lawson sells weed
to juniors who go to our school,

while Lawson sells weed
to sophomores who go to our school,

while Lawson sells weed
to freshmen who go to our school.

'Til Lawson stops, asks,
"How old are you?" to
two kids in polo shirts and baseball hats.
They say, "Thirteen."

"Get the fuck outta here," Lawson says,
"I don't sell to kids."

in the park

we sit on a bench.
I do my homework,
while Lawson smokes another menthol.

"You see that guy?"
"What guy?"
"Guy over my shoulder."
"Yeah. What about him?"
"He looking at us?"
"Kinda."
Lawson closes my book,
shoves it in my backpack,
says,
"Let's get outta here.
He could be Five-O."
"Five-O?"
"A cop."

i park

María Carmen in my driveway.
Before I get out,
I kiss her steering wheel,
whispering, "*Gracias.*"

"Why you do that every time?"
Lawson asks.
"*For luck,*" I say,
"*so she keeps working for me.*"
Lawson laughs.
"You stupid."

We
(real quick)
bump fists,
shake hands,
bump shoulders.

"*See ya, dude.*"
"Later, broseph."

Lawson starts
to walk across the street
to his place,
then stops
and turns back.
"You ain't stupid.
I shouldn't'a said that."

"*I am sometimes.*"

He says, "Not often."

my house

smells like lemons
and there's no dust anywhere.

That's Mom's doing,
taking pride in our home,
even if boards creak,
even if faucets leak,
even if it isn't ours,

'cause we can't afford
to own a home
not with the money we make
no matter how hard we work.

All day
Mom cleans hotel rooms,
cleans homes,
then
comes home
and cleans our home,
dustless and citrus scented.

Mom says,
"Idle hands are the devil's playground.
And I don't want a drink."

I say,
"*At least let me vacuum.*"
Mom asks,
"Have you finished your homework?"

"*Not yet.*"

"Finish studying.
        That's more important."

slipping me two twenties,

Lawson winks.
I ask,
"*What's this for?*"
"For driving me 'round."

I push the forty bucks back to him.
"*Keep it.*"
Lawson puts his hands up.
"I don't want it. It's yours."
"*You already paid for gas yesterday.*"
"I pay for gas, but I gotta pay for your time too."
"*Dude. You don't gotta pay me.*"
"You help me, I help you."

"*But I don't want your—*"

"My what?"

"*Your . . . you know . . .
drug money.*"

Lawson looks
like I hit him.

He takes the cash,
rips it in half,
lets it go,
bits drifting
to the ground
like autumn leaves.

"*What'd you do that for?!*"

"If you don't want it, it's gone."
"*Don't do that.*"
"Either you take it, or I trash it."
"*Fine. Next time, I'll take it.*"

Lawson looks at the torn bills on the ground.
"You gonna pick that up?"

I do.
When I get home, I look for tape.

"come on,"

Lawson says.

*"Nah. I'll just wait here
in the car."*

"And do what?"

"Read my book."

"What book?"

"Franz Kafka's Metamorphosis.*"*

"What's it 'bout?"

"This guy wakes up one day, and he's a giant insect."

"What kind?"

"Doesn't say. I think a cockroach."

"That's some sci-fi shit right there.
But save your homework for later.
Come inside.
It'll only take five minutes."

her tweed couch

is itchy.
Christina is itchy too.
She keeps scratching her arm
between puffs from a cigarette
gripped between her teeth like a toothpick.

In the corner,
some guy
named Frank
inhales storms of white smoke from a water bong,
his eyes barely open.

The TV plays cartoons on mute.
The stereo plays Led Zeppelin.
Musty fumes hang in the air.
The curtain's closed,
making the room
feel like a cave.

On the coffee table
is a mountain of weed,
and a cardboard box of plastic baggies.

Christina takes
a stick of sticky green
with several blooms
of stinky bud,
puts it in a clear bag,
puts the bag in a pile of bags.

I sit there,
waiting,
so Lawson can get the drugs,
and we can leave.

Lawson notices a book on the table.
"My brother here likes to read,"
he says. "He's reading a book now
'bout a guy turns into a roach."

"A roach you can smoke?"
Franks asks.
"Nah, a cockroach."
"It'd be better if he turned into a joint,"
Frank says,
"a giant joint."

"*Clever*,"
I say, sarcastic.
Lawson shoves my shoulder.
"Don't be a dick."

"Can you imagine?" Christina says,
"A person-sized joint."

Lawson laughs.
So does Christina.
I don't.

But Frank
finds it hysterical
and can't
stop
laughing,
while he hugs
his bong
like a teddy bear.

dime bags

don't cost 10 cents.
They cost 10 bucks.

How much weed
you get?
That depends
on Christina.

rolling a joint

goes like this.

Lawson grinds
bud
in a grinder
so his fingers
don't get sticky
and stick to the rolling paper.

From a tiny book,
takes a tiny paper square
as thin as a page from the Bible.

Adds a filter
then the shake,
sprinkling bud on the square
like sugar on a cookie.

His magic fingers
catch the bottom edge and twist,
tucking into the green,
then rolls.
Pinching the sides,
rolls it
back and forth,
packing the weed down,
back and forth,
puts it in a dollar bill, rolling it,
back and forth,
rolling rolling rolling
'til it's tight.

Lawson licks the paper's side,
folding it over,
sealing it with a final roll.
He packs the end of the joint
so he has an even burn and . . .
    . . . voilà!

He holds it up
like a trophy
and smiles,
proud.

He flips the joint toward the sky,
catching it on his lips,

and lights up.

high time

is not normal time.
It's a lot slower.
I'm waiting for Lawson
to get his weed
so we can leave,
but Christina
is taking
her
own
sweet
time,
minutes
one
by
one
by
one
drifting,
dragging,
stretching,
as if
they'll
never
run
out.

I realize
I shoulda stayed in María Carmen
with Kafka.

the whole time

I'm there,
I'm watching the clock
on the wall,
my antsy knee
bouncing up and down
nervous.
Lawson punches my leg,
"Cut it out,"

but I can't.

I keep waiting for
the cops
to kick open the door
swarm the room,
shove us down,
cheeks pressed into crusty carpet
screaming,
"Hands behind your head,"
then handcuffing my wrists,
adding,
"You have the right to remain silent,"

even though I'm already silent,
when maybe
maybe
I should speak up
and say,
"*I'm gonna go wait in the car.*"

right when

I think we're about to leave,
Christina's phone rings.
She answers,
whites of her eyes
growing wide
saying
calmly,
"I'll get it, Trent.
I'll get you the money."

Christina's face
turns pale.
Her lips
with a slight quiver
saying,
"Yeah. By Monday.
Yeah.
I promise."

When she hangs up the phone,
she says,
"Fuck fuck fuck."

I ask, "*Is everything okay?*"

She yells,
"Mind your own goddamn business!"

when we leave

I stomp toward the car
all in a huff.
Lawson asks,
"Why you mad?"

"'Cause that took forever.
You said five minutes."
"Five minutes is a figure of speech."

"Fuck that, Lawson.
I have shit to do."
"Reading 'bout dudes
turning into bugs?"

"Yes. I gotta write a paper on it."
"Why didn't you say so?"

"So now it's my fault?"
"You need to chill.
Ain't no thang.
Relax."

But it is a thing.

And it's hard
to relax
when you have
your whole future
resting on every grade,
your whole future
resting on every mistake,
your whole future
waiting
for
you
to make it happen

                    or fuck it up.

"munchies, munchies, munchies,"

Lawson says,
pointing at a 7-Eleven.

I park the car,
so Lawson can buy

Kit-Kat
Snickers
Starburst
Gummy bears
Laffy Taffy
Ruffles Cheddar & Sour Cream potato chips
Chili Cheese Fritos
a cold 20-ounce Dr. Pepper
and
a pint
of Neapolitan
Blue Bell ice cream
(chocolate, vanilla, and strawberry
in brown and white and pink).

"You're eating all sugar.
You should really eat something more healthy.
Like an apple or banana.
Maybe get a salad."

"I don't do fruits and veggies.
That shit's for rich people.
And when I'm high?
I eat what I want."

Lawson starts eating,
finishes it all before we get home,
except the gummy bears
he's still chewing
and chewing
and chewing
as he giggles
at nothin'.

a lottery ticket

only costs a buck.
So I buy it
for Mom,
hoping it'll win
and give her a million dollars.

When I hand it to her,
she says,
"In the future,
don't waste your money.
Every dollar you save,
is a dollar you can spend later
on college
or a new car
or a house for your family."

She adds,
"Some people play the lottery.
I save my dollars
to gamble on you.

You're a good bet."

mom rubs her feet

sitting in her chair,
watching the news,
with a glass of iced sun tea
next to her,
while I make a simple meal
of pollo y arroz.

"Mom,
you work too hard."
"Life is work.
And work is good.
At least I have a job.
I thank God every day for it."

After dinner,
I go to my room,
sit cross-legged
on my bed,
open my math book,
and start my homework.

If Mom can work hard
at her age,
I can work hard
at my age
too.

at work

I bus tables,
putting plates
and forks
and cups
(painted with the remains
of food, coffee, and syrup)
into black tubs,
then carry them back
past the kitchen
into the dishwashing room,
where I scrape wasted food
into a trash can,
put the plates in a tray
to run through the dishwasher,
which breathes warm hot humid wet air
like an angry water dragon
'til it spits out the tray
with clean plates
and forks
and cups,
ready to go to the kitchen,
where they will be used again,
and I will bus again,
and wash again,
in a never-ending cycle.

At the end of every shift
I stink
of old food.

I get why Lawson sells drugs
rather
than bus tables.

But,
I tell myself,
at least with this job,
I can't get arrested.

when i step out

I'm wearing
dirty shoes
holes in them,
jeans baggy
holes in them,
used shirt
from Goodwill,
backpack
that I've had since middle school,
with stains on it.

When Lawson steps out,
he's wearing
new shoes
bright white,
jeans baggy
brand new,
new shirts,
new polos,
new jacket,
gold chains
around his neck
matching
gold earrings
with tiny diamonds in them.
He looks pimp.
OG.

And I look broke.

Which I am.

Am I jealous?

I'd be lying if I said no.

"you ever worry,"
I ask,
"*about cops? Or getting arrested?*"

Lawson shakes his head.
"I'm seventeen.
Worse they can do is put me in juvie."
"*Your birthday's coming up.*
You can be tried as an adult."
"I ain't eighteen yet."
"*You gonna stop dealing when you're eighteen?*"

Lawson shakes his head.
"Probably not."

two girls

stop by our table
lean over
so the tops of their breasts
say hello.

"Hey Lawson."
"Hey Lori. Hey Vanessa."
"You going to Davey's party this weekend?"
"You gonna be there?" Lawson asks.
Lori lifts her pearl necklace to her mouth,
bites it,
and nods.
Her designer skirt,
brand name top,
real leather purse
and stainless new shoes,
I suspect
all cost more
than my entire wardrobe, combined.

Lawson says,
"If you there,
I'm there."
"Cool," Lori says.
The two girls walk away
giggling.

"They like me," Lawson says.
I say, "*Everyone likes you.*"
"You know why?"
"*Why?*"
"'Cause folks like a little danger."

"*Someone should tell them,
danger is a bad thing.*"

Lawson shrugs,
saying,

"Life
       is danger.

It's just more dangerous for some
                        than for others."

at the party

I sit on the couch
drinking my ginger ale
watching kids my age
have fun.

Lawson is making the rounds
with his secret handshake
(different from our
bump fists, handshake, shoulder bump)
'til he runs outta weed to sell.

Then he makes a
beeline for Lori
and kisses her neck
in the kitchen doorway
'til they start
making out.

She pulls back,
giggles,
makes eyes at him,
asking,
"You have any weed left for me?"

He holds up a joint.
"You know I do."

Lori and Lawson
join me on the couch,
smoking dope.
Lori tries to pass the joint to me.
"You want a puff?"
"I'm good."
"Dude, come on.
Be cool.
Smoke with us."
"Nah, I'm fine."
She says,
"Loser."

"He ain't a loser,"
Lawson barks at her,
like an angry dog,
before adding,
"Benny's tight.
He just don't smoke."

Lori says, "Seems like a square to me."

Lawson yanks the joint outta her hand.
"You wanna smoke my weed,
don't rag on Benny."

Lori snaps,
"Seriously?"

Lawson says,
"Seriously."

"Whatever."
She gets up and storms off.

"You don't gotta defend me."

"Yeah, I do,"
he says.
"Bros before hoes."

when i come home

Mom sniffs the air,
says,
"I smell weed."

"I was at a party.
Everyone was smoking,
everyone except me.
So don't worry."
"I do worry.
Don't ruin your future."
"I'm not. I didn't smoke."
"Did Lawson smoke?"

I don't like lying to Mom.
So I don't say anything.

"I don't like Lawson.
I never have,
you know that.
He's bad for you."
"He's my best friend."
"Then you need new friends."

Suddenly
I'm shouting,
"No, I don't.
Lawson's always been there for me!"

Mom breathes deep
so she can speak calmly.
"He'll get you into trouble,
like I used to get into trouble."

I'm shouting,
"No one can get me in trouble
except me."

Mom nods.
"You're right.
Your choices are your own."

She goes to her room,
and softly
closes the door.

NOVEMBER

when he calls

Lawson asks, "You free?"
"For what?"
"I need a ride."
"I'm busy."
"Doing what?"
"Reading."
"Whatcha reading now?"
"Kurt Vonnegut. Slaughterhouse-Five.*"*
"What's it 'bout?"
"This guy gets unstuck in time, and bounces back and forth all through his life."
"Sounds like a bad trip."

Then he asks,
"You wanna do acid this weekend?"
"I have homework."
"You always have homework."
Lawson hangs up.

over at lawson's

we play Grand Theft Auto
on his PlayStation.
Fingers punching buttons,
thumbs moving joysticks,
stealing cars,
shooting people,
dodging cops,
giving crime
and death
not a second thought.

After all,
it's just a game . . .

right?

lawson's mom

comes home,
cigarette hanging on her lip
like a thermometer,
saying,
"Heya, boys."

Colleen goes to the fridge,
eyes the interior,
asks,
"Where's my beer, Lawson?"
Lawson, still playing the game,
not taking his eyes off the screen, answers,
"You drank it."
She slams the fridge closed.
"Yeah, right."

"I didn't drink that lite shit," Lawson says,
"I buy my own beer."

"Why'm I not surprised?" she says,
stubbing out one cigarette,
trading it for another.
"How's school?"

"Whatdya think?"
Lawson says,
focused on driving a stolen car.

"Why can't you be more like Benny?"

"*My grades aren't that good,*" I say.
Lawson whispers, "Liar."
"*I can help you study.*"
"I'm good."

"Lawson," Colleen says,
her voice slower, lower,
sitting softly on the couch.
"I'm behind on rent."

Lawson pauses the game,
puts down the controller,
without looking,
asks,
"How much?"

Colleen says,
"Four hun-erd."
Lawson reaches into his pocket,
retrieves a roll of twenties,
counts . . . sixteen, seventeen, eighteen, nineteen, twenty
twenty-dollar bills,
gives them to his mom.

She kisses him on the cheek,
saying,
"Thank you."

She doesn't ask where he got the money.
She knows.

I wonder if she cares.

two kids coming down the hall

take one look at Lawson,
the first saying,
"Wigger."

Lawson says,
"And proud of it."

Another looks at me,
says,
"Trailer trash."

Quick as a tiger,
Lawson is on top of him,
hitting
hitting
hitting
hitting him

'til I'm pulling him off.
Lawson shouting,
"Don't say shit 'bout Benny,
or I'll do worse next time."

"why you pissed off?"

Lawson asks.
"I'm the one got suspended."

"*I can fight my own fights,*"
I snap.

"You and me?
We look out for each other.
Right?"

I don't say nothin'.
He asks again,
"Right?"

"Right."

"Now come on.
I need a ride."

back at christina's

I'm sitting outside
in María Carmen,
windows down,
reading.
Lawson comes out
with a backpack
he didn't have
when he went in.
He asks,
"Whatcha reading?"
"Aldous Huxley's Brave New World.*"*
"What's it 'bout?"
*"This guy lives in a future where everyone does drugs all the time to
make them feel better."*
"Sounds like paradise."
"It isn't."
"Wanna see somethin' cool?"
Lawson opens his backpack
showing me
a brick
of weed
wrapped
in clear Saran wrap
as if it were a loaf
of banana bread.

"I'm not driving you anywhere with that."
"I'll put it in your trunk."
"Fuck no."
"I'll stick it under the seat then."
"No fucking way."
"Whatdya want me to do?"
"Take a bus. Call a cab. I don't care. That's not coming in my car."
"Christina needs me to move this for Trent."
"Move it without my car."
Lawson gets out,
slams the door.
"Fuck you."

I drive off,
still sweating, being that close,
to that much of something
illegal.

six days

Lawson doesn't talk to me.

He doesn't call.
He doesn't come over.
He doesn't sit with me at lunch.
He doesn't talk to me in the hallways.

On the seventh day,
he calls me
says,

"I need a ride."

"chill out,"

Lawson says,
"We're just going to Lori's."

I ask again,
"What's in the backpack?"
"Books, man."
"Show me."
He opens his backpack.
I dig around.
Just textbooks.
"Sorry,"
I say,
even though
I don't know why
I'm the one apologizing.

After he gives me directions,
I drive.
"Why we going to Lori's?"
"To study."
"You don't study."
"She don't know that."
He smiles.
"Quickest way
into a girl's panties
is to ask her for help studying."

Lawson turns the radio up,
singing
"Ooh-la-la"
along with the Fugees
"Ooh la la la la la la lalala la lah"
'til
I'm smiling
and singing too.

"i need a ride,"

Lawson says,
"over to the college."
"For what?"
"Whatdya think?"

He doesn't have a backpack,
but I know his
pockets are full

and
what

they
are
full
of.

so i sit
on a bench,
doing my homework,
while he sells weed
to seniors who go to this college,

while he sells weed
to juniors who go to this college,

while he sells weed
to sophomores who go to this college,

while he sells weed
to freshmen who go to this college.

'Til he comes back
to find me
pissed off,
throwing my books
into my backpack.
He asks,
"What crawled up your ass this time?"
And I'm shouting,
"*You said one hour.*"
"Yeah, well, shit happens."
"*Yeah, well, I'm late for work.*

Selfish asshole."

my boss
shouts,
spit
coming outta his mouth
hitting my cheek
screaming about me being late
but I don't say nothin',
except,
"*I'm sorry.*
It won't happen again."

Even though
        I know
            it will.

my paycheck
barely covers
my gas
and
car insurance.

Have I mentioned?
I hate my job.

a hundred dollars

is what Lawson hands me
saying,
"For driving me 'round last two weeks."

I'm about to say no,
but the five twenties
weigh heavy
in my hand

but
feel lighter
in my pocket.

I already know
I'll deposit it
in my bank account
and use it next year
when I get
to college.

she's walking my way

and I try not to look
try not to make eye contact
with a junkie
that makes the world
a little bit darker,
sadder,
inside my heart.

She sees me
see her,
walks up to my car,
holds out empty, dirty hands
syringe punctures
dotting the crook of her arm like ants,
and she asks,
"You got a few bucks?"
I shake my head no,
even though I do,
making me feel
dense with guilt
like I could be her
under different
circumstances.

As she turns to walk away,
I say, "*Wait*,"
fishing out a crisp, clean
ten-dollar bill
from my pocket,
and hand it to her.
"This is for food, okay? Food."
She says,
"Sure."

Mom sees this
as she comes outta the post office.
In the car, she shakes her head,
"You shouldn't give her your money.
She'll spend it on drugs."

I say, "*Maybe she won't.*"
Mom says,
"She will."

lori's throwing a party

while her parents are outta town.
The walls are tall and white,
windows floor to ceiling,
everything brand new,
polished to shine,
like it's all saying,
you'll never have this.

Everyone who's anyone
from our high school
is there.
I'm there with Lawson,
who for once
takes the night off.

It's Lawson's birthday.

Today he turns eighteen,
legally an adult,
who can vote in his country
who can die for his country
who can buy cigarettes
(but not alcohol)
and go to jail if he gets caught
running drugs . . .

But I don't wanna think about that.

lawson and lori

are macking down
for everyone to see
with reckless
abandon
as if they're in love
or just full of teenage lust.

Lawson has always gotten the girls
with ease.
He has mad game.

It's harder for me
since I don't have
his charisma
his charm
his looks.

I try to remind myself
he has girls
but I have good grades
and the possibility
of a bright
future.

But when I think about Lawson's fate,
this dark cloud
wells up inside me
like a weight
in my stomach
worried
about what he'll do
if I leave town
(when I leave town)

                    without him.

"i need a favor,"

Lawson shouts
over the drum
of the loud music
when he comes
to sit by me.
"I want you to smoke with me."

"I don't smoke. You know that."
"Just this once," he says,
"just one hit."
I shake my head, no.
He says,
"For my birthday."

I stare at the joint
for a long time.

He says,
"Come on, broseph.
Just one hit."

"One hit?"

"One hit."

I don't wanna.
Except I do.
I always have.
Wanted to try it.
Just to try it.
Just once.

It's Lawson's birthday.

I take the joint,
and inhale

too deep.

i cough

over and over
and over and
over and over
again
'til tears
run down my cheeks
and Lawson says,
"Atta boy."

Lawson gulps down
the contents
of his red plastic cup
saying,
"Let's ditch this shithole."

"What about Lori?"

Lawson smiles.
"Girls?
Always leave 'em wanting more."

at waffle house

we are eating
breakfast at midnight
when I notice
hash browns
have never tasted
this good
which makes me
laugh
and laugh
and laugh.

Lawson says,
"You are stoned."
I say,
"*Yeah I am.*"

even though i shouldn't

I drive us
(real slow)
to the edge of town
to the old lake
that's dried up
and gone.
We lie
on the hood
of María Carmen
staring up
at the stars
in the sky
winking back at us.
Twinkle
       twinkle
             little star.

Lawson says,
"I wish I was you sometimes."
"Me?"
"Yeah, you. You see anyone else out here?"
"Why?"
"'Cause of how you are.
Walking the straight path, reading books and shit, having
this whole big
          future
               ahead of you."

"You can have that too."
"No, I can't.
It's too much work for me."

"It's the same amount for me."
"No, it ain't. You got smarts."
"No, I really don't. I gotta work really hard for every single grade I get."
"See? That. You got that.
Whatever that is inside you
makes you work hard,
I ain't got that."

"You can."

"Then why am I failing half my classes?"

"'Cause you're too busy selling.
Too busy chasing girls.
Too busy smoking."

"Maybe I'll stop,"
Lawson says.

"Which part?"

"Not the girls,"
Lawson laughs.
"Smoking the 420."

"Yeah?"
"Yeah."

Lawson looks up at the stars.
"Yeah.
I need a clear mind.
I'm gonna quit smoking weed."

the very next day

Lawson shows up
on my doorstep, ready
for his ride to school
with red eyes
and a sleepy
faraway
look.

"I thought you were gonna stop smoking?"
"When did I say that?"
"Last night."

He snorts.

"You can't hold me accountable
for anything I say
when I'm stoned."

"wake and bake,"

Lawson says,
when I ask
how he's already stoned
at 8 in the morning.

"Wake up,
toke some smoke.
Makes school easier.
Less stressful,
I mean.
Makes things more funny too."

He smiles.
"I just don't remember nothin'."

"take a few days off,"

I say,
my words a challenge
to joust, to duel,
on principle.
Lawson doesn't like being cornered.
To soften the blow, I add,
"*Start with one day.*
Twenty-four hours."

Lawson presses his lips together.
"Why would I do that?"
"To see if you can."
"I can if I wanna.
I just don't wanna."
"So then you can't."
"Yes, I can."
"Prove it."
Lawson gets real mad

but

reaches over
hand out
and
shakes on it.

DECEMBER

"seven days,"

Lawson says,
"and I ain't smoked once."
I say,
"*That's really awesome.*
I'm impressed."
Which
really
I am.

"Know how I'm gonna celebrate?"
Lawson says.
"With a joint."

"just kidding,"
Lawson laughs
and laughs.
"The look on your face," he says,
poking my cheek,
"like you're your mother or somethin',
all disappointed
and shit."

*"Seven days is awesome.
Think you can do thirty?"*

"Maybe.
We'll see.
No promises."

I know I'm pushing it
but I say it anyway,
"You could stop selling."

Lawson scrunches up his face
like he smells something rank.
"Why would I do that?"

"lemme show you somethin',"

he says,
pulling a Nike shoe box
out from under an Adidas shoe box
hiding at the back of his closet.

He opens the lid,
showing me rows
of rolls
of tens and twenties
wound over themselves
like massive, fat joints
made of cash.

"You ain't gonna make this
busing tables at no diner,"
Lawson says.
"Ain't no one our age
making this kinda dough.
So stop selling?

Nah.

I'm good."

i'm at another party
on the couch
with my ginger ale
watching folks
having fun
while
I'm thinking
I should be studying.

Lawson is making rounds,
shaking hands
only this time,
I notice
the little baggies
aren't filled with

    green bud

but with

    white powder.

outta the bathroom

Lawson walks
with Lori,
both of them
wiping their noses
over and over,
making sure
the powder
doesn't show.

I grab Lawson's arm
asking,
"*What're you doing?*"

Lawson yanks his arm back.
"It's just a little coke.
Calm down."

"*You said
you were gonna stop doing drugs this month.*"

"No,
I said
I was gonna stop smoking weed this month.
I didn't say nothin'
'bout anything else."

"*So now you're selling coke?
What the fuck, dude?*"

Lori laughs.
"Lawson can do what he wants.
You're not his father."

"*No, I'm not his father.
I'm better.
I'm his brother.*"

Lori asks,
"You two are related?"

"No,"
Lawson says,
eyes cold at me,
"we're not."

cocaine

Blow.
Snow.
Coke.
Coco.
Crack.
Sniff.
Sneeze.
Speedball.
Nose candy.
Eight ball.
Big C.
Little C.
Dust.
Flake.
Pearl.

Folks like to sniff them
Lines.
Rails.
Snort
      those
            bumps.

I'm judging.
That shit can't be good for you
going straight to your brain
eating through
your nose cavity
like sugar
eating through teeth.

My best friend, Lawson, he's snorting coke.

Selling it too.

"find your own ride home,"

I snap,
walking outta the party,
the air so cold
I can see my breath.

"Don't be a dick,"
Lawson shouts
after me.

I slide inside María Carmen
when Lawson grabs my door
holds it open,
saying,
"It's no big deal.
Don't be so dramatic."

"I don't want you selling that shit.
And I definitely don't want that shit in my car."

"It's not in your car.
It's in my pocket."

"I drove you here.
Meaning, you had it on you
and didn't tell me."

"I don't need to tell you every goddamn little thing.
Shit. It's better if I don't.
That way,
you can't get in trouble
if anything happens.
You know I'd never let you take the fall."

I . . .

I do know that.

Don't I?

"come on,"

Lawson says,
trying to open
the passenger side door
except I won't unlock it.

I put the car in drive
about to take off
when Lawson runs in front of
María Carmen,
stands there,
defiant
in my headlights
like a glowing angel
surrounded by darkness
without wings to fly away.
His eyes,
they're not angry,
they're hurt.

"Don't be like that," he says.
"Just give me a ride home."

*"I told you,
that shit isn't coming in my car."*

"The coke? It's all gone."

"I saw you snorting it."

"Yeah, and I sold the rest.
You can check my pockets."

He takes off his jacket,
despite the cold,
and holds it out for me.
"Go on. Check it."

I sit inside the car.
He stands outside,

shaking his jacket for me to inspect,
saying, "You gonna let me in? It's fucking cold out here."

Thoughts wrestle in my head
one voice saying,
"*What're you doing? Drive away.*"
The other saying,
"*He's your brother. Let him in.*"

Finally,
I unlock the door.
Lawson jogs around and hops in.
He punches me in the shoulder.
"Good man."

i can't sleep
all night
keep tossing
and turning
and turning
and tossing
worrying
that Lawson is gonna fuck up
his
whole
entire

life.

I don't wanna see him behind bars.

I don't wanna see me behind bars either.

all I can think about
lately
is two things:

#1:
my college applications,
if I'm gonna
get in.

#2:
Lawson dealing
and if he's gonna
get caught.

mom asks,

"How's school going?"
"Fine,"
I say.
"If I pass my exams,
even with a B or C,
I'll still make all A's this semester."
She says,
"You will.
Keep studying.
I'm proud of you.
You'll get into college.
You'll be the first in our family to go.
You'll make something of yourself."

"I hope so."

"Just think.
In ten years,
you could be a doctor
or a lawyer
or anything you want.
In ten years,
you will look back
and all the hard work
will be worth it."

In ten years,
I wonder
if Lawson
will still be selling,

and more importantly
if
we'll still
be
brothers.

they say

best friends
grow apart
after high school
especially when
one goes to college
and the other stays behind.

It's always in movies and on TV and stuff.

But Lawson and I won't be like that.

Ten years of friendship
can't end
like that.

It just can't.

Right?

in my sleep

I dream
of Lawson
only he's not him
he's a bear
his foot
caught
in a metal trap
with metal teeth
clamped onto his leg,
as blood streams out
and he bellows
in agony.

I approach slowly
put up my hand
to calm him.
Instead,
he roars at me
gnashing his teeth
not letting me get near
swiping his giant paw and claws
in my direction

I keep trying
but he won't let me
come close enough

to help him

even though
he doesn't know how
to escape
himself,

which

leaves him

trapped.

"i need a ride,"

Lawson says,
"I'm just selling some weed
to a couple of old folks
in an old folks' home."

"Yeah, sure."

"I'm serious,"
he says,
"Christina hooked me up
with a nurse who works there.
I sell to him,
he sells to them,
helps them have a good time,
which they need.
You ever seen a place like that?
It's fucking depressing."

I wanna
but
I don't believe Lawson.

I drive him anyway.

At the senior center
he hangs outside the back door
'til it opens
and he sells weed
to a nurse.

"It's practically charity,"
Lawson says,
getting back in my car.

"Except you're getting paid."

"Yeah,
but I'm still doing a good deed.
Think of all them old folks

all happy and toked up,
slurping that pudding,
maybe even a little horny."

I can't help but laugh.

for christmas

Lawson and I
have this tradition
where he comes over
and we watch
A Christmas Story.
You know, that movie
with the sexy leg lamp
and that kid who wants a BB gun
even though
everyone keeps saying,
"You'll shoot your eye out."

Every holiday,
my mom cooks:
a honey ham
cornbread stuffing (from a Stove Top box)
mashed potatoes
and
green bean casserole
(from a recipe
on the back of a Campbell's
Cream of Mushroom aluminum can)
with extra French's Crispy Fried Onions
(my favorite),
and then
we eat
and eat
and eat
'til our stomachs ache
but still
we want dessert.

This year,
Lawson changes
the tradition
by showing up . . .

     as
        a
          kite.

super stoned

Lawson lies
on the living room carpet
asking,
"When's the food gonna be ready?"
during the commercials
between parts of the movie on TV,
which makes Lawson
laugh and
laugh and
laugh.

Mom asks me,
"Can I see you
in the kitchen?"

When it's
the two of us,
she asks,
"Is Lawson on drugs?"

I don't know what to say,
so I lie,
"*Of course not.*"

"He is,"
Mom says.
"I'm not stupid.
He has to leave."

"*Mom—*"

"I don't want drugs in our house."

"*You can't kick him out.
He always spends Christmas with us.
He doesn't have anywhere else to go.*"

"He can go to his own house
across the street."

"And eat what?
His mom isn't even home."

"That's not my problem.
He can't stay here."

I stand firm.
"If he goes, I go too."

Mom looks as though
I struck her

and the way she looks at me,
I feel like
I did.

She says,
"Then that's your choice.
You choose."

I can spend Christmas with
my brother
or
my mother.

But
     I
         can't
              choose
                       both.

"*i love you,*"

I say,
kissing Mom on the forehead,
"*but I can't let Lawson*
be alone,
not today."

"So instead,"
Mom says,
"I'll be alone."

Torn
but choosing
brother over mother,
stomach sick,
I walk
                away
into the living room,
and nudge Lawson with my foot.
"*Come on. We gotta go.*"

"What about the food?"

"*We're on our own this year.*"

luckily

a Chinese restaurant
is open.

We do not order the duck
like in *A Christmas Story*.

Instead,
we order:
egg drop soup
fried egg rolls
crispy wontons
pepper steak
orange chicken
honey shrimp
and so much rice
and then
we eat
and eat
and eat
'til our stomachs ache
but still
we want dessert.

But all they have
                  are fortune cookies.

my fortune says

"Salt and sugar
look the same."

lawson's cookie?

It doesn't have a fortune in it.

"what now?"

I ask.

Lawson says,
"Let's go to Lori's,
her parents just left
to visit her grandmother."

Once we get there,
I sit on the couch,
while Lawson disappears
upstairs with Lori.
I can hear her giggling,
while I sit downstairs
watching *A Christmas Story*
by myself,
thinking about
Mom
at home

alone

with the ham.

i ditch
Lawson
and drive home
in María Carmen,
the car Mom gave me,
hoping it's not too late
to make things right
with her.

When I get home,
Mom is gone.

A note on the counter
says,
"Leftovers are in the fridge."

For some reason,
this makes me
wanna cry.

i am dreaming

on the couch
where I fell asleep,
worried,
watching TV
waiting for Mom
to come home
when the phone rings.

Leaping up,
I grab the phone
saying,
"*Hello?*"

Mom says,
her words slurring together,
"I need a ride."

"merry christmas, asshole,"

Mom says,
getting in the car
from the bar
where I picked her up.
She giggles at nothin'
then looks out the window,
her smile fading
away.

The rest of the ride we're silent.

When we get home,
I half carry her toward her bedroom,
when she bolts
for the bathroom
and vomits
on the floor
after missing the toilet.

I will clean it up later.

For now,
I rub her back,
tell her it'll be okay
'til she is ready
to crawl toward her bed
while I help her up,
take her shoes off,
tuck a sheet over her,
and pull a quilt
(that her mother sewed by hand)
up to her chin,
her heavy eyes blinking at me,
like she's waiting for a bedtime story.

She starts crying.

"Don't be like me,"
she says.

"Be better."

the next day

Lawson
knocks at my window
through the metal bars
that are supposed to keep intruders out
even though they also
keep us
locked in.

"Whatcha doing?
"Reading."
"What book now?"
"Shakespeare's Hamlet.*"*
"I know that one. 'Bout that guy wants revenge on his mom and her
boyfriend for killing his pops."
"You read it?"
"Nah. Watched the movie in class."

This long
silence
stretches
between us.

"I just wanted to say,
you know,

                        thanks,

for yesterday,
for choosing me
               over your mom.
She mad?"

"She won't even look at me."

"She'll get over it.
You're a good kid."

"I hope so."
"So . . . "
"So . . . "
"Yeah."

"You need a ride?"

"Nah. I'm taking the day off.
Wanna come over and play video games?"

playing video games

makes me feel
like we're kids again.
Racing cars,
shooting aliens,
using mushrooms to make us grow
and feathers to make us fly.

We laugh

about nothin'

in particular.

I wish

I could

stretch

this moment

out

so

it

would

last

forever.

"i almost forgot,"

Lawson says,
pulling something from his pocket,
hands it to me.
"Got somethin' for you.
For Christmas."

"We said no presents."
Lawson shrugs,
"I lied."

Wrapped in newspaper
is an empty box of Kool menthols
still smelling of tobacco
that contains
five hundred dollars
served
in five
one-hundred-dollar bills.

"I can't take this."
"Yes, you can."
"Lawson. I can't."

"You can and you will.
It's for your college fund.
You're going.
I ain't.
You'll need it."

I think of tuition
of textbooks
of paper and pens
of all the things I will need
to make my future happen.

But I push the money back.
*"Lawson, please.
I don't need a present."*

"Don't insult me, Benny.
Just take the money.
If you don't wanna spend it on you,
use it
to bail me outta jail."

"*That's not funny*," I say.

"Who's joking?
My life? That's a joke.
And I'm the punch line.
One of these days,
I'll end up in prison.
Or
if I'm lucky,
on a farm
growing weed
and smoking it up
'til I die."

*"Don't say that.
I hate when you say shit like that."*

"Benny. Take the money.
Please."

Not able to say no,
I put the money
in my pocket
saying,
"*Thank you, Lawson.
I mean it.*"

Even
as I
try
not
to think
about where

the money
came from

even
though
I
already
know.

driving

down the street
I notice stained tents
and leaning shanties
made of wooden crates
and cardboard
and tarps,
all put up on sidewalks
with old chairs and plastic bags and dolls and radios
junk for the junkies
that makes homes
for the homeless
more homey.

I remind myself
to be grateful
for having a roof over my head
for having three meals a day
for Mom,
who never stops
encouraging me
to do better,
even when she stumbles.

But I keep thinking about the users
and wonder
how long
before Lawson
        is selling
        to them.

But he wouldn't do that.

Would he?

"you ever gonna talk to me again?"
I ask Mom
after cornering her in the kitchen
after days of being ignored
after she stopped
looking at me,
her only son.

Her eyes
can't meet mine
as she whispers,
"I'm so embarrassed."

I hug her
as she starts to cry,
'til she's sobbing.

When the tears taper off,
I ask,
"*Have you talked to your sponsor?*"
She nods.
"He wants me to start going to meetings again."
"*I think that's a good idea.*"
"It means I have to leave work early,
which means less money for a while."

"*I'll pick up extra shifts.
Whatever we gotta do
for you to get better,
we'll make it work.*"

She says,
"I'll need a ride.
Can you drive me?"

new year's eve
is finally here
and I'm looking forward
(as cheesy as it is)
to watching the ball

                             drop

in New York City
while I'm hundreds of miles away
at home
watching TV
on the couch.

Instead,
Lawson says,
"We're going to a party."

The big bash is at the house
of someone I don't know,
named Kincaid,
who graduated
from our high school
like eight years ago.
As soon
as we walk in
Kincaid asks Lawson,
"You invite some girls?"
"Yeah," Lawson says.
Kincaid makes his fingers
look like a longhorn
and shakes it,
adding with a smirk,
"I love high school girls."

Already
I wanna leave.

the party

is made up of
Kincaid,
a few guys in their twenties,
a woman in her thirties,
a couple of college students,
a waitress,
a cashier,
a few high school seniors,
Lori,
Lawson,
                    and me.

I'm glad
for a table
with four bags of Cheetos,
some Oreo and Chips Ahoy! cookies,
and an open two-liter bottle of ginger ale
so that I can snack
while
everyone gets high,
smoking water bongs,
snorting coke,
'til
Kincaid brings out
four orange plastic
prescription bottles,
dumps them on the
glass coffee table,
and says,
"Pill party time."

There are
round pills
square pills
oval pills.
There are
white pills
blue pills
pink pills.

There are
capsules
of red and white
white and blue
yellow and white.

Each has its own set
of tiny letters
and numbers,
though no one
seems to know
what any of them mean.

"Take one at random,"
Kincaid says,
"and be surprised."

Lori takes one.
Lawson takes one.
Everyone takes one

                    except me.

I say,
"*I'm good.*"

Lawson sighs,
saying, "Really?"

"Really."

"Your loss, dude,"
he says,
tosses the pill in his mouth,
and swallows.

i shoulda
stayed home.

Instead
I sit
in a metal folding chair
watching the ball
                        fall
surrounded by people
chatting nonstop
or half asleep
while Lori
can't stop crying
for no reason.

at midnight

everyone
(who is still awake)
cheers
and
claps.

After Lawson
kisses Lori,
he pats me on the back
saying,
"Happy New Year, brother.
This year
is gonna be the best year
                              ever."

I hope it is
I really do
but all I can think about
is the missing fortune
in Lawson's cookie.

JANUARY

"fuck this place,"

Lawson says,
hopping in my car after school,
slamming the door.
"Ms. Duncan says I ain't gonna pass
if I make the same grades
as last semester."

"You're smarter than that,"
I say.
"You gotta try."

"Why?"
"So you can graduate."

"Then what?"

We're both quiet.

"maybe I'll drop out,"

he says,
"and sell full-time."

My stomach
tightens
and drops,
sick
at the thought
of Lawson
doing
what he's been doing,
'cause there's no future in it.

Not one that I can see,
and
definitely not one
that has a happy ending.

"make a deal with me,"

I say.
"Stay in school.
Make a real effort.
Work toward graduating.
And I'll keep driving you around."

Lawson pauses.

"If I don't?"
"No more rides."
"Bullshit."
"Try me."

Lawson hesitates.

"A real effort,"
I say.
"You gotta do your homework,
and study for tests.
I'll help you."

Lawson hesitates
again.

"If you want me to drive you . . . "

He rolls his eyes,
breathes out
annoyed
but still
offers me his hand.

"Deal."

then he pulls out a joint
holding it
between thumb and the next finger,
and prepares to light up.

"What're you doing?"
I snap.
"You stopped smoking weed."

"For thirty days,"
he says.
"Thirty days is over."

"you know the rules,"

I say.
"You can smoke,
but not in María Carmen."

Lawson grunts,
gets outta the car
closes the door
then leans back in
through the open window
to say,

"Yes, Mom."

when i get home

from an early weekend shift
at the diner
to take Mom to a meeting
I find her bedroom door
closed.

I knock.
"Mom?"
I hear movement
on the other side of the door
when something hits the ground
with a soft thud
and Mom says,
"Shit!"

Inside,
I find Mom
on her knees
picking up a bottle of Jim Beam
as it spills
soaking
into the carpet.

Starting to cry,
Mom says,
"I'm sorry,
I'm so sorry.
I just needed a drink.
Everything is just too hard.
You don't understand what it's like."

I say,
"*I don't.*
But I can help.
Let me help you."

I walk Mom
to the kitchen
where her hand is shaking

over the sink
as she pours
the rest of the whiskey
down the drain.

when i'm called outta class

to the principal's office,
my heart stops
beating.

I'm six years old again
being led down a hall
for putting pink gum
in Trisha Holden's curly permed hair.

I'm ten years old
being led down a hall
for being caught
showing my test answers to Adam Garcia.

I'm thirteen years old
being led down a hall
for belting Tommy Starks
in the face when he called my mom trash.

Those times,
I knew
I was in trouble,
'cause I knew what I did.

This time,
this is worse,
'cause this time,
I don't.

I am seventeen years old
walking alone down an empty hall
except for the rows of lockers
staring at me
like a row of accusers
in silence
vibrating red
with judgment.

My mind spins,
asking,

> *What'd I do?*

all tough,

she sits
at her desk
in her office,
lit dim except a lamp
shining on a wood placard,
its black name plate engraved in gold
that says Principal Alexandra Villalobos.

Hair pulled back tight,
red-rimmed glasses
reflecting a computer screen,
while her short unpainted nails
click and clack against the keyboard keys
before she finally looks up,
face unreadable.

"I'm concerned,"
she says.
"I've noticed you run around with Lawson Pierce."

Knots
interrupt my stomach,
my breath catching in my throat,
imagining what Mom is going to say
when I tell her everything went sideways.

"*Yeah*," I say.

"He's a bad element at our school.
Bad grades. Poor attendance.
Suspended every other month for how he talks to teachers."

I say, "*Yeah*."

"Why do you hang with him?"

I shrug.
Contemplate
even though I already know.

"We grew up together.
He's my best friend."

"You should reconsider
who you consider
a friend."
She says, "You have a bright future, Diego.
I'd hate to see you mess it up."

I stare down
at the linoleum floor
between my shoes.

She says,
"Congratulations.
You rank twelfth
out of the whole senior class."

My stomach releases
its butterflies,
letting them
fly away
toward the sun in the sky.

"I'm telling you this," she says,
"because you have to keep it up the rest of the school year.
You have to focus,
double down,
do whatever you can.
Work hard,
and maybe you can make top ten."

"But Lawson," she adds,
"don't let him be a bad influence."

The first thing I do
is ignore the last thing she said
'cause all I want to do
is tell Lawson
the good news.

But when I see him,
I stop,
reconsidering,
not wanting to rub it in,

that I
      might actually
                  get outta this town.

lawson is kissing lori

at her locker,
saying, "I'm so proud of you, baby girl."

When he sees me,
he squeezes my shoulder,
asking,
"Did you hear?"
"Hear what?"
"Lori. She's a—
whatdya call it?"

"Salutatorian," she says.
"It means
out of the whole class,
I'm number two."

This makes me feel stupid,
'cause I didn't know
what salutatorian meant,
even though I knew
valedictorian means number one.

And I'm surprised,
no . . .
shocked
when I find out Lori ranks above me.

Lori lifts her pearl necklace
from neck to mouth
and bites,
white teeth on white beads,
then claps her fingertips in little claps
wearing a purple cashmere sweater and plaid skirt
and a purse
with brand names
I could never afford.

Lawson asks me, "Can you believe it?"
I say, "*I really can't.*"

"What's that supposed to mean?" Lori asks.
"I just . . . I thought you were a party girl."
Lori shrugs,
saying,
"Work hard, play hard."

Lawson kisses her neck.
She giggles.

Between my job,
my homework,
school,
hanging with Lawson,
every hour of every day is stolen,
I don't have a free minute to my name.
I wonder out loud,
"How do you do it?
Balance everything?
When do you find the time?"
"I make time," Lori says.
"You have to have fun in life."

It feels
like a kick in the gut,
making me question
if I'm doing everything

                         wrong.

after lori walks off to class

Lawson's shoulder
bumps into my shoulder.
He says,
"Don't be jealous."
"*I'm not*," I sneer,
my face burning hot.
"Yeah you are.
I know that look."
"*I'm not jealous,*
I'm envious."

Lawson rolls his eyes.
"Same difference.
But look.
Her dad makes bank.
She has two parents.
And tutors.
A maid.
A yoga instructor.
Her own life coach,
whatever the fuck that is.
It's easy for her.

"You, though,
you work hard.
Your hands are rougher
than hers will ever be.
That's not a bad thing.
Get what I'm saying?"

"*I do, yeah. But I don't gotta like it.*
Some people start with everything.
Other folks?
We get nothin'.
Doesn't seem fair."

"Yeah, well,"
Lawson says,

"the universe?
Never said it was fair.

It doesn't owe us a goddamned thing."

when i get home

I sit at the table
doing my homework
'til Mom comes out
looking tired
(and thirsty
for the wrong kinda drink).

"How was your day?" she asks,
'til she sees my face.
"You're grinning ear to ear.
What's going on?"
I get up,
give her a hug.
"*Number twelve,*"
I say,
"*in the whole class.*
I'm number twelve."

Mom stares at my face,
'til it sinks in.
She asks,
"Twelve?"

I nod.
She squeals,
squeezing her arms
around me.

We spend the next quarter hour
jumping, laughing,
dancing around the living room
to music
playing only in our heads
that sounds
like a good future
is coming
for us.

friday night

Lawson vanishes
as soon as we get to the party
he dragged me to.

Now
I'm sitting on a long couch,
drinking ginger ale,
watching kids
drinking beer
from a keg
(sometimes upside down),
howling with laughter,
or singing lyrics
to the newest pop song
playing on the stereo,
everyone
letting loose.

I wanna have fun too,
let go of everything,
maybe I could loosen up
maybe if I just have a couple drinks . . .

But I think of Mom.

But then,

then I think of Lori
saying,
"Work hard, play hard."

I work hard.
Maybe I should play,
not hard,
but
maybe
just
a little bit.

To celebrate.

Just this once.

naked,

four guys jog through Johnson's party
drinking from red cups
hollering, "Wooooooo,"
dongs and balls
flopping around
like
well . . .
dongs and balls.

One guy slams into another partygoer,
who falls backward,
crashing through a wooden coffee table.
Everyone goes silent
'til he raises his hand,
still holding his red cup of beer
unspilled
and says,
"I'm okay."
Everyone cheers.

I wanna be okay too.
Not through-a-coffee-table okay,
but laughing okay.
Having fun okay.
One drink okay.

So I go into the kitchen,
and pour vodka
in my ginger ale.

I'll just have one.

Mom'll never know.

vodka

tastes like
the way I imagine
rubbing alcohol
tastes like.

I swallow it down,
ready to have a good time too.

i find myself

actually talking
to a girl,
Lori's friend
Vanessa,
who I've never talked to
even though
we're in the same English class.
We talk
about books,
about our teacher,
about whatever comes to mind.

While I've been drinking,
I haven't seen Lawson,
assuming he's doing his magic tricks,
exchanging powder
and grass
for cash
'til

Lawson and Lori come downstairs
arguing,
though their raised voices
are lost among the music.
She slaps a baggie outta his hands.
Lawson launches
onto hands and knees to grab it back
before it's stepped on
by the shoes of his peers
while Lori storms off.
Then Lawson storms toward me,
grabbing my arm, saying,
"Time to go."

"No. I'm having fun."
"I ain't."

My words come out
all smooshed together,
"*Well, I can't drive.*"

Lawson looks at me,
impressed.
"Finally."
I feel a crooked smirk
crawl across my face
proud
that Lawson is proud
since neither of us has fathers
to be proud of us.

"Fuck it," he says. "Let's get hammered."
I shake my head.
"*No.*
You can't."
Handing him the keys to María Carmen,
I slur,
"*You gotta be responsible tonight.*
'cause
I'll need a ride . . .

but

not

just

yet.

I'm having fun."

I take another drink.

underwater

I let myself sink
to the bottom of the pool
breath held tight in my lungs
in a world lit only by small shimmers
that waver and dance
with the slightest movement   ·
everything radiant blue
beneath a mirrored surface
dangling with tangles
of bodies
with legs and feet kicking
while arms and hands wave
to tread water,
my peers headless,
their faces on the other side
above the water

all of them night-swimming

while I float

down

here

weightless

                              at peace

when i wake up

on Lawson's couch,
my head is aching
as if split
and shattered
like a dropped watermelon.

Lawson hands me a cup of coffee,
saying, "Drink this."

He ruffles my hair,
chuckling,
"Last night, you were a wild man."

"Why are my clothes wet?"

"You jumped into Johnson's pool,
fully dressed."

It comes back slow
my recall
of the night before.

For a few hours,
I was one of them,
just another teenage kid.

But now,
it is
back to reality.

"i was worried sick,"

Mom says,
bags under her eyes,
'cause she hasn't slept a wink.
"How am I supposed to trust you
when you start acting like Lawson?"

"*It was one party,*" I say.
"*I go to parties all the time.*
And I'm always responsible."

"But you don't stay out all night,
And you don't come home reeking of booze."

"*I needed to do it.*
Just once.
Just to see what it's like.
To be like everyone else."

"You mean, like me?"
"*No. Of course not.*
I just wanted to feel like a . . .
like a teenager."

"Diego. I'm an alcoholic.
And it's a disease.
A disease that runs in our family.
I don't want you to go down that road."

"*Mom. I won't.*"

Mom crosses her arms,
hugging herself tight
wanting to trust me.
Finally,
she asks,
"Was it worth it?"

I can't help but grin.

on monday at school

some kid I barely recall from the party
nods in class, giving me a knowing look,
Johnson gives me a high-five in the hallway,
and Vanessa
sits next to me in English,
giving me a wink,
filling me with awe
at how one night
changes things.

"crime and punishment,"

I answer,
"*by Fyodor Dostoevsky,*"
after Lawson asks what I'm reading.
"That 'bout cops?"
"*Nah. This guy plans to kill this old woman
to get ahead in life.
He's trying to convince himself
the ends justify the means.*"

Lawson says, "Sometimes they do.
Sometimes you gotta do bad things
for good reasons.
Like selling
to put food on the table."

"*And what about the people who get hurt in the process?*"

"I sell weed.
No one ever got hurt
from getting stoned.
More people get hurt from drinking
and I don't sell alcohol."

Unfortunately,
statistics show,
that's the truth.

I can't argue with the truth.

drumming his pencil

against the pages,
Lawson leans over
his textbook
then writes something
in his notebook.

He's actually studying.

after an hour

he shuts his book,
saying,
"Aight.
I'm all learned up.
I need a ride."

lawson knocks

at Christina's front door.

Me, I pull out my homework,
ready to sit here, waiting for an hour
while Lawson does what he does.

Lawson knocks again.
Then again.
He cups his hand
to look in the windows.

I'm watching
as Lawson opens the front door
and slips inside.

I wait,
minute after
tense minute,
worried about what he's gonna find.

When he comes back,
he says,
"She's gone.
Looks like she left in a hurry."

I'm thinking,
that can't be good.

Or maybe,

maybe
this is the best thing
to happen to Lawson
in a long time.

FEBRUARY

lori and lawson are holding hands

in the hallway
as he walks her to class
before kissing her, sending her off
to make her straight A's
on her way
to valedictorian.

I ask,
"*You two official?*"

"Yup," he says.
"She's like you, you know.
Makes me wanna be a better person.
Stay outta trouble."

"*Does that mean—?*"

Lawson rolls his eyes.

"Nah.
I said it makes me
want
to be better.

Didn't say I would be."

at the lunch table

Lawson seems bothered,
his eyes focused
on nothin'.

I ask, "*What's going on?*"

"Christina's been gone a week,"
Lawson says.
"She's not answering my calls.
How can I deal without a supplier?"

"*Maybe now is a good time to—*"
"Don't say it."

"*Don't you have enough
money saved up to last you a while?
Take a break.
Concentrate on school.*"

"Maybe," Lawson says.

I guess

maybe

is better than no.

"whatcha reading?"

Only this time
it's me asking Lawson
about the book in his hands.
"*Outsiders.*"
"*What's it about?*"
I ask,
even though
I've already read it.

"'Bout this kid,
Ponyboy, stupid name,
but I guess he's in a gang,
called the greasers
'cause they're poor.
It's kinda cool.
For a homework book."

This big warmth runs through me.
Glad. Pleased really.
Like someone in Lawson's life
should be.

'Til Lawson
tosses the book
over his shoulder,
saying,
"I need a ride."

"*Where now?*"

"Trent called me.
I'm back in business."

i'm waiting outside

a Church of Christ church
in a rough neighborhood,
overgrown fences
lawns with weeds
most of the homes
falling apart
little
by little.

Sitting in María Carmen,
I have the overhead light on
textbook in my lap
pencil in hand
writing answers to homework,
having sat here for an hour
while Mom does what she needs to do
at her meeting
with others
struggling
not to drink.

Lost deep inside
my physics homework
I jump sideways,
startled,
when Mom knocks on my window
and smiles.

When she gets in the car,
she leans over,
hugs me,
kisses me on the forehead
and says,
"Thanks for the ride."

i'm waiting outside

a two-story house
in a nice neighborhood,
all green lawns
and every home
a mirror image
of the one
next to it
just
with different shades of beige.

Sitting in María Carmen,
I stare at my textbook,
ready to sit here for an hour
while Lawson does what he does.

Lost deep inside
my trigonometry homework
I jump sideways,
startled,
when someone knocks on my window.

The man is huge,
like a linebacker,
tattoos cover his arms
disappearing into his shirt
then crawl outta his collar
and up his neck.

He says,
"Lawson says come inside."
"I'm good out here."
He opens the door, grabs me by my shirt,
says, "Get outta the car,"
but doesn't wait for me,
hauling me out,
and pushing me toward the house.

My heart
        bah-bum, bah-bum, bah-bum

pounds
entering a dark living room,
blinds closed,
my eyes trying to adjust
from the bright sunlight outside.
A girl is curled up, passed out on the end of a sectional,
down three cushions
from Lawson, who sits uncomfortably,

naked
except white briefs and white socks,

across from a lean man with a teardrop tattooed under one eye.

"What're you doing outside?"
the stranger asks.
"*Homework*," I say.
Tear Drop laughs.
Then
his smile vanishes,
saying, "Check him."

The tattooed giant wrestles my shirt off,
baring my chest to the room,
scanning my torso
then my back,
then says, "Take off your pants."
"What?"
"Take off your fucking pants,"
Tear Drop says.
Lawson says,
a pleading look in his gaze,
"Just take 'em off."

Slow
I unbuckle,
unzip,
drop trou,
and let the linebacker
survey me, up and down.

"He's clean," he says
as if expecting to find
(I realize)
a wire.

Tear Drop leans back,
relaxing,
saying,
"I don't like people sitting outside my house."

i'm sitting

next to Lawson,
naked too
except plaid boxers and black socks,
wondering
what the fuck is gonna happen next.
Lawson says,
"Trent, look—"
but the lean man with the teardrop tat
silences him with a hand gesture.

"No. You look," Trent says.
"You worked for Christina,
who worked for me.
Now she's gone,
so you're moving up the food chain.
Think of it as a promotion."

"What's that mean?" Lawson asks.

"You're selling double what you were,"
Trent says, examining his fingernails.
"Up to you if you wanna outsource.
But more drugs means more pay.
You in?"

Lawson asks,
"Do I get to say no?"

Trent places a gun on the coffee table.
He says,

"No."

i'm still shaking

ten minutes later when
I pull my car over into the city park
where Lawson sometimes sells.

I throw open the door,
leap out,
storm through the grass,
up to a tree,
where I punch it with my fist,
again and again
trying to get the fear out
'til my knuckles are bleeding.

Lawson paces after me,
calmly,
asking, "You okay?"
and I'm screaming,
"*No,*
I'm not okay!
What the fuck was that?"

"That was Trent," Lawson says.
"Guess I work for him now."

"*Fucking quit, dude.*
That guy is scary as shit.
I'm never driving you back there," I shout.
"*Never.*
I mean it.
I fucking mean it."

I hit the tree again,
leaving my blood
on the bark.

"*Fuck Trent.*
No more selling.
You're gonna get caught.
Or hurt."

"Not if I'm careful," Lawson says,
"and I'm always careful."

"I bet a lot of people say that
before they get found out."

"Trust me, okay?
You trust me, don'tchu?"

"I trust you.
But
you can't control circumstance,
you can't control what the universe does,
and you can't make this into a career.
It won't last. It's too risky.
You gotta find something else.
Get a real job."

"A real job?
In this town?
You mean flipping burgers?
Stocking groceries?
Busing tables?
I need to make money.
Real cash money."

"You can make real money
with a real job."

"And it'll take five times as long.
Or longer.
I need quick funds.
I gotta take care of my mom.
I gotta pay the bills.
I gotta pay rent."

"Your mom can pay—"

"No, she can't!"
Lawson shouts.

"She can't even get a job!
I'm the man of the house.
It's my job to take care of shit.
I gotta do this!
I don't have any other choice!"

I wanna say he does.

But
I don't know
if that's true

or just
what
society
tells us.

"i need you,"

Lawson says
in the park,
us surrounded by nature
lush trees and green grass
that you can't smoke
but can walk around on
barefoot.

Lawson says,
"I don't have a car.
I can't get 'round without you.
And you made me a deal.
I'm trying at school.
Really trying.
Studying and shit.
We shook on it."

I feel sick,
my stomach
in knots
tossing
and turning
and turning
and tossing
'til I wanna throw up.
But I don't.
I hold it down.

"You gotta help me out,"
Lawson says.

"Come on.
I'm begging."

i have mom

but Lawson doesn't
have anybody
like that.

His grandparents long dead.
His mom on welfare.
His dad gone.

Like mine.
Like me,
Lawson is an only child.

I have Mom,
but Lawson?

He

just

has

    me.

i whisper,

"*You don't gotta beg.*"
Then,
after a minute,
add,
"*But I don't wanna know shit about it.*"

He says,
"I won't tell you a goddamned thing."

"*If something happens—*"
"It won't."

We stand there
for a while
in a green park, under blue sky
'til an ache arrives in my knuckles
pain settling in
from attacking the tree.

Lawson raises his hand
(real slow)
waiting
'til I raise mine too
and we
bump fists,
shake hands,
bump shoulders.

I notice
my blood
on Lawson's hands

and suspect

no . . .
                    I know

this

this is a mistake.

don't ask, don't tell.
That's our policy now.
Even though Lawson and I
never said it out loud.

I wanna believe
I'm smarter than this.

So why do I keep driving Lawson?

'Cause we were friends since we were kids.
'Cause he's always been there for me.
'Cause he doesn't have anyone else.
'Cause I need to be there for him.
'Cause he's my ride-or-die.
'Cause he's my brother.

Take your pick.

on valentine's day

Lori kisses Lawson in the hallway,
and walks him to class.

After he disappears
inside a classroom
Lori sees me,
walks my way,
and says,
"At least he's in school.
I have you to thank for that,
don't I?"

"No thanks necessary."

She says,
"He's lucky to have you."

When she walks away,
I begin to wonder

if the reverse is true.

Am I lucky to Lawson?

Or just the opposite?

"i need a ride,"

Lawson says on the phone.
"I can't. I have work tonight."
"Blow it off."
"You know I can't."
"You can't. Or you won't?"
"Either way."
"I'll pay you double what they pay you at that shit diner."

Not gonna lie . . .
I'm tempted.

But I can't lose this job
no matter how much I hate it.
"I'm sorry, dude. I really can't."

"Then I ain't studying,"
Lawson snaps.

"I'll drive you tomorrow."

"Whatever."
Lawson hangs up.

"you have to stop hanging out with lawson,"

Mom says.
I come back,
"*You always say that.*"
"I mean it this time."
"*Why?*"
Mom hesitates,
even though she's burning to say something,
but worried it'll piss me off.
"I saw . . .
I saw some people at his house yesterday."
"*You saw some people?*"
"They looked shady. Like bad news."
"*And?*"
"They were in and out.
Who goes inside someone's house for five minutes,
then leaves?"
"*So you're spying on Lawson now?*"
"Just trust me. A mother's intuition never lies."
I grab my coat.
"Where are you going?"
"*Over there. To ask him.*"
"You think he's going to tell you the truth?"

"*He always does,*"
I say,

though at the same time
curious
and wondering:

He always tells me the truth . . .

doesn't he?

"you dealing outta your house now?"
I ask
as soon as I walk in Lawson's front door.

Lawson takes a toke from a joint,
inhales through gritted teeth,
saying, "Just a one-time thing.
I needed cash
pronto."

"Are you stupid?"
I shove him.
He falls back onto his couch,
chuckling.
I snap,
"You don't shit where you eat.
You know that.
You're smarter than that."

Lawson shrugs.
"Why you so mad?"

"'Cause!" I'm shouting.
"'Cause why?"
"'Cause I don't want you to fuck up.
All it takes is one mistake,
and you go to jail for the rest of your life."

Lawson
has no smirk on his face.

"I won't do it again,"
he says
under his breath,
"but you know what that means."

"Yeah, yeah.
You need a ride."

sometimes
after school
Lawson gets a ride home from Lori.
But today,
walking to María Carmen,
I see Lori yelling at Lawson
in the parking lot

'til she gets in her new Mercedes,
slams the door shut,
and peels out.

Lawson kicks the truck tire next to him
then punches the side.

I drive over slowly
and ask,
"You need a ride?"

Lawson gets in,
huffs.

"What was that about?"

"You know girls,"
Lawson grumbles.
"They're never happy."

"You do something to piss her off?"

"Who knows?"
Lawson says.
"Wanna blow off some steam?"

"Whatdya have in mind?"

Lawson smiles.
"Mario Kart."

these?

These are my favorite times
with Lawson
these days,
just us,
controllers in hand
racing cars
trying to beat each other
to come in first
and win the gold.

All we do is laugh.

That's when
I look over at him,
his body language
his face
his eyes,
              and I see him.

He's no longer
a drug dealer.

He's just
the boy
he was

before life
came along
and insisted
he be a man

in a hard world.

"i need to talk to you,"

Lori says,
pulling me aside in the school hallway.
"Lawson won't listen to me.
Maybe he'll listen to you."

"What're you talking about?"

"It's one thing to sell weed.
It's another thing to sell the hard stuff."

"You were fine to snort it when he first started selling coke."

"I'm not talking about just the cocaine."
"What do you mean?"
Lori studies my face,
then says,
"You don't know?
About what he's selling now?"

"What is he selling?"
"Besides weed and coke?
         Acid. Xanax. Ecstasy."

I'm thinking
Fuck.
Fuck fuck fuck
                    fuck.

"I didn't know."
I didn't.
Don't ask, don't tell,
remember?
What was I fucking thinking?

"Will you talk to him?"
Lori asks.

"I care for Lawson. I really do.
I don't want to see him ruin his whole life."

Her voice is my voice.

I say, "*Yeah, I'll talk to him.*"
"Good," she says. "If he won't listen to his girlfriend,
maybe he'll listen to his brother."

acid

LSD.
Alice.
Angels in the sky.
Blotter.
Dots.
Micro-dots.
Mellow yellow.
Windowpane.
Hats.
Hits.
Golf balls.
Goofy.
Loony toons.
Lucy in the sky (with diamonds).
Mother of god.
Pizza.
Purple haze.
Teddy bears.
Sunshine.
Zen.

Comes in a dropper,
or served up on tiny squares of paper,
or soaked into Smarties,
SweeTarts,
or Pez.

Folks like to drop it on their tongues
and take off
for parts unknown
their bodies left behind
like a hermit crab's forgotten shell.

My best friend, Lawson, I don't know if he's taking it.

But he's selling it.

xanax

Xannies.
Bars.
Z-bars.
Zanbars.
Handlebars.
Planks.
Totem poles.
School bus.
Bicycle parts.
Footballs.
Blue footballs.
Yellow boys.
White boys.
White girls.
Benzos.
Upjohn.

Folks like to pop them
pills,
or take a whole bar
that looks like the long
four-block rectangle
from Tetris.

I'm judging.
That shit makes you all tired
confused
quiet
like you're just waiting to die.

My best friend, Lawson, I don't know if he's taking it.

But he's selling it.

ecstasy

MDMA.
X.
E.
Eve.
Go.
Hugz drug.
Lover's speed.
White Mitsubishi.
Biscuit.
Beans.
Adam.
Clarity.
Disco.
Peace.

Folks like to swallow it down
and
dance dance dance
'til they're grinding their teeth,
or sucking on pacifiers.

I'm not gonna lie,
I've always been curious.
But I'd never do it.
Sure, I wanna feel good.
Even just for a little while.
But I won't.
I won't risk it.
Not with my future coming.

My best friend, Lawson, I don't know if he's taking it.

But he's selling it

        along with everything else.

this is bad.
Real bad.

like every day

Lawson walks through
the parking lot
after school
saying hi to this guy and that girl
shaking hands
along the way.

Like most afternoons,
Lawson meets at my car,
hops inside,
asking me,
"How was your day?"

Today
I ask,
"What's in your pockets?"

"Nothin'. Why?"

"What's in your goddamned pockets?"
I launch myself at him
then we're wrestling,
me trying to get my hands
inside the pockets
of his puffy coat.
Shoving my elbow
into his neck
he grabs at it
forgetting his defense
as I slip my hands inside
and pull out two dozen little baggies,
full of pills and bars and tiny pieces of paper.

"What the fuck?"
I'm shouting.
"What the fuck, Lawson?!"

"I told you I wouldn't tell you.
You can't get in trouble if you don't know."

"Why are you doing this?"
I'm roaring
'til he matches my fury
and roars back,
"You know why!"

"No, I don't!"

"'Cause Trent told me to!"
he shouts,

then
adds,
in almost a whisper,

"Trent isn't a guy

        you can say no to."

"call the cops,"
I say,
"*turn him in.*"

"He'd find out,"
Lawson says.
"I'd be a dead man."

"*You gotta stop.
You gotta get outta this.*"

"How?"

"*I . . .
I don't know.*"

Lawson,
he says,

"Neither do I."

at the diner

I am stuck
in an endless loop
picking up dirty plates
placing them in bus tubs
putting them in the dishwasher
restacking them in the kitchen,
where more food will be placed on them
and sent out to the customers
who will eat
pay
and leave,
leaving me to pick up the same dishes
all
over
again

like Sisyphus
rolling the rock
up the mountain.

I remind myself,
soon I will be in college,
and I won't have to do this anymore.

I will escape this life
to start a new one.

But is this,
I ask myself,
the fate I want for Lawson?
Stuck in a shit town with a shit job and going nowhere?

How can I help free him
from the trap
this world
has built
for him?

"whatcha reading?"

Lawson asks
at the cafeteria table
when he sits down across from me.
I don't look up.
"Joseph Conrad. Heart of Darkness."
"What's it 'bout?"
"Do you care?"

"How long you gonna be like this?
You haven't talked to me in days."
"You gotta stop selling."
"You gotta quit nagging me.
You sound like Lori."
"Good. 'Cause we both care what happens to you."

"We had a deal.
I stay in school, I study, I make an effort,
you drive me.
That's what you said."
"I can't help you peddle drugs.
Weed was one thing. But this shit?
It's dangerous.
And it's wrong."

"I ain't selling anything but recreation.
People don't abuse this stuff.
No one gets addicted to acid."
"How about Xanax?"
"Shit, man. You gotta stop."
"No, dude. You gotta stop."

Lawson growls,
"A real friend wouldn't turn his back on me like you."

"That's where you're wrong.
A real friend would do everything in his power to stop you
from going down this road you're on.
And I'm trying to do that
I've been trying to do that all year.

What do I gotta do
What do I gotta say
to get it through your thick skull
that selling
is gonna end you.

"I'm your brother
Whether you like it or not.
And brothers look out for each other.

The way
      you
          aren't
               looking out
                    for me."

I don't realize I'm shouting
'til the cafeteria turns quiet
as hundreds of pairs of eyes
fall on us.

Standing, Lawson, crimson-faced,
snaps,
"What'd you say?
I've done nothin' but look out for you.
Our whole lives I've been there.
For you."

"*'Til now,*"
I snap back,
unable to contain my furious tongue.
"This year's been all about you,
me driving you around
like a goddamned chauffeur
risking my whole future
so you can sell drugs.
And for what?
What's your plan?
What're you gonna do with your life?! Huh?!"

Silence stretches out
filling the space,
building a wall
between us
as the rest of our peers watch
two brothers battle
with eyes
without words
'til Lawson speaks, saying,

"Benny. Fuck you."

"No, Lawson. Fuck you."

Lawson's fists crash into the table.

He turns
so all I can see
is his back.

He doesn't turn around
before he disappears
through the doors

leaving me
wondering

if this is it
for us.

MARCH

two weeks

I've never
gone this long
not talking to Lawson.

It feels final.
Like this might be the end.
Ten years of friendship.
Gone like nothin'.

This abyss
opens in my chest
threatening
                    to swallow
                                    me
                                        whole

'cause I lost Lawson.

And
it's
all
my
fault.

at school

when Lori passes Lawson in the hallway,
he doesn't even look at her.

When I pass Lawson in the hallway
he doesn't even look at me
his eyes turn away
like he's avoiding staring
at the blast of a nuclear bomb
so he doesn't see
something he doesn't wanna see.

I know why he's mad.

So why do I feel guilty?

part of me
thought
with Lawson gone
I'd have more free time.

But
I still have

school

homework

work at the diner

taking Mom to AA meetings

trying to find time to eat and shower and

sleep
even if it is only six hours a night
or sometimes
less

'cause
free time?

Some people have it.

                    And some people

                              don't.

in my gut
there is this
tension
like a rock
no, a boulder
heavy and solid
weighing me down
like gravity has turned against me
just 'cause
I'm trying
to have
hope
that despite evidence

Lawson is okay.

Even if he never
talks to me again
I want him to live
a long
and happy
life.

But to do that
he's gotta stop selling
and start
living

even if it means
giving up all that easy money
that has a price tag
bigger
than he can see.

it's almost midnight

when the phone rings.

"Hello?"

There's a long silence that stretches out.

"Hello?"

A heavy breath on the other end.

"Who is this?"

Then Lawson stammers into the phone.

"I, uh . . . I got the shit kicked outta me."

I've only heard it twice before
but Lawson's in pain,
fighting back tears,
hurt bad.

"How bad is it?"

"I need a ride."

"who was that?"

Mom asks, sleepy,
coming outta her room
as I'm getting my shoes on.

"Lawson. He needs me."

"Stay home, Diego.
No good can come of this."

*"Mom, I gotta go.
He's hurt."*

"Hurt how?"

*"I don't know.
But I need to help him."*

"Your future—"

*"—isn't going anywhere
'cause I choose to help someone."*

"That's where you're wrong,"
Mom shouts after me.
"You can't dance with fire
and not get burned."

I don't mean to
but
I slam the door behind me.

bright red blood

drips down
from a deep cut
across Lawson's brow,
and from his nose,
and from his lips,
dripping
down his chin
ruining his white shirt,
when my headlights find him
sitting on a curb.

He's slow to get up.
When he does,
he stumbles,
and falls.

Jumping outta the car,
I run to his side,
helping him stand.
Lawson tries to take a step,
his leg gives out
and I catch him.

"I'm okay,"
Lawson says.
"Just bruises. Nothin' broken. I think."

"We should take you to the hospital to get checked out."
"No!" he snaps, then calmly,
"They'll ask questions."

"What happened?"
"Got jumped," Lawson says.
"Guess I was selling on someone else's turf.
Said the south side was theirs
then beat my ass to a pulp."

His arm around my neck,
I carry him

depositing him
into the safety of María Carmen,
maybe the only place
he doesn't have to be hard,
the only place
he can just be himself.
Then
I notice
the color of his blood
matches the color of my seats.

his face

is a kaleidoscope
of color:
red
and blue
and yellow.
Luckily
the swelling
has gone down
after a few days
and Lawson can walk
without limping

too much.

"you gonna stop now?"

I ask later.
"Stop?" Lawson says. "I can't.
Those fucks stole the cash and pills I had on me.
I gotta pay it back to Trent
outta my own pocket."

"*Shit, Lawson, I'm sorry,*"
I say,
even though
I don't know why I'm apologizing.

"Wouldn't have happened
if you were driving me."

Or it would have happened to both of us,
I wanna say
but don't.

"I was waiting for a cab
when they jumped me," Lawson says.
Ever heard of a dealer taking a cab to his clients?"

"*You could take the crosstown bus.
Like my mom.*"

Face scrunched,
Lawson shakes his head,
no.

"*Then ride around on a bicycle.
A pink one with little tassels on the handlebars.
Maybe you could get one of those little braided baskets up front,
keep your supply in it.*"

Lawson,
he cracks a smile.

Already,
everything feels lighter.

lori

is holding Lawson's hand at school again.

When Lawson walks past,
arm around his girl,
he winks at me.

I know what he's thinking.

"No girl
can resist
a man
bruised and broken."

lawson knocks at my window

"Whatcha reading?" he asks.

"Candide, *by Voltaire.*"

"Sounds fancy as fuck."

"It's about this dude, starts his life all good,
practically in paradise
then everything goes bad,
and just gets worse and worse."

"Does it have a happy ending?"

"I don't know yet.
I haven't finished it.
What's up?"

"I need a ride,"
Lawson says.

"Lawson—"

He shoves a paper test
through the bars on my window
with his name on it
marked
with a letter grade
of a B.

"I studied.
I passed.
You owe me."

we hit up

a college party
where Lori and Vanessa
are dancing on a table
in synch with throbbing music.

Lawson lifts Lori off,
giving her a big kiss
placing her on the ground
while I help Vanessa.

I give her my hand
and she accepts,
stepping from table
to chair,
and trips
into my arms
with a laugh as light as air.

Lori asks Lawson,
"Is that a blunt in your pocket
or are you just happy to see me?"

Lawson smirks,
pulling out a weed-stuffed cigar
from his new black denim jeans.

Lori lights it up, inhales.

"Puff puff pass," Lawson says,
and Lori holds it up for him
to take a drag.

Lori holds it up for Vanessa
who turns it down
making me like her
even more.

Lawson says something to Vanessa,
though I can't hear
over the mix of party noise.

Lori catches me eyeing her,
leans over, and says into my ear
so I can hear
despite the roar of music,
"I'm not a hypocrite.
I don't do the hard stuff,
but I like to drink and smoke."

"I didn't say anything."
"You didn't have to," she says,
pointing the blunt at me,
"I know what you're thinking."
"I doubt that very much."
"You're thinking,
why does Lori even like Lawson?"
*"And if I was
thinking that?"*
"Look. The heart wants what the heart wants."
"So you really care about him?"
"I do."
"Despite what he does."
"Despite what he does,"
she says.
"But I hope he stops.
Sooner rather than later."

Lawson interrupts us
asking,
"Who wants a drink?"

in the kitchen
just me and Lawson,
he asks,
"What you and Lori gossiping 'bout?"
"You."
Lawson shrugs.
"Cool."
He pours whiskey into a red plastic cup
adds coke
(soda, not powder)
and takes a glug.

Lawson asks,
"Wanna know what I was talking 'bout with Vanessa?"
"Should I?"
"She likes you, you tool."
"Yeah right."
"She does. You should ask her out.
Or at least find a dark corner and make out with her."
"You're all class."
"Classy as they come," Lawson says.

We return
to the girls,
offering them up
plastic cups of wine
(from boxes)
as requested.

Vanessa takes my hand, saying,
"Come with me."

we sit on wooden stairs

outside the party,
watching people come and go
while Vanessa drinks cheap wine,
and I drink ginger ale.

"Why do you hang out with Lawson?"
"He's my best friend."
"But you two are so different."

"We're not that different."
"But you're, like, this amazing student.
Not far behind Lori."
"How would you know that?"
"Rumor has it."
I shrug
not wanting to brag
but still saying,
"*The rumors are true.*"
"See? You have a future, and Lawson—"
"Don't."
"Don't what?"
"Say it."
"He's a drug dealer, Benny."
"He's doing what he has to do."
"And you?"

"I'm doing what I gotta do too,

               just on a different path."

lawson holds back lori's hair

while she pukes
into a bush
outside the party
while Vanessa
rubs Lori's back,
asking,
"How much did you drink?"
Lori cries, apologizing, saying,
"You don't know how stressful it is,
being me.
My dad wants a perfect daughter,
and I'm trying,
I'm trying so fucking hard
but salutatorian isn't good enough for him."

Then she pukes again.

Vanessa turns to me,
asking,
"Can you give us a ride home?"

"please,"

I say,
"please,
don't puke in my car."
So Lori hangs her head outside the window
air pushing her hair
'til she lets
what's inside
go outside.
Then she does it again.

She moans,
"Lawson, don't look at me like this."

Lawson in the front seat,
trying not to laugh,
says,
"You have puke on your chin,"
and starts laughing.
I smack his arm.
"Don't be a dick."

When we get to Vanessa's,
she hops outta the seat behind me,
closes the door,
leans in through my open window
kisses me on the cheek
and says,
"Thanks for the ride."

She jogs around the front,
moving through headlights
taking Lori from Lawson,
to help her inside.

Lawson waves bye,
then hops in the car.
"Got a kiss, huh?"
"*Shut up*,"
I say,

even as
        I start
            to smile.

car wash quarters

roll outta the machine
into my hand.

Under fluorescent lights
that break the dark of midnight,
I spray the side of my car
with water
to wash away
what looks like chunks
of spaghetti.

Lawson says,
"You hungry? I feel like pasta."

So I spray Lawson.

He chases me,
like a dog chasing a cat,
the water tube from the ceiling
spinning around and around.

Finally, Lawson tuckers out,
leans against a wet wall, huffing,
while I take the soapy brush,
scrubbing the puke
off the side of María Carmen,

washing away the past,

and hoping

for a fresh start.

cruising
through town
under a sky
missing its moon
everything all black
except the neon lights
of storefronts
and streetlights,
one of them flickering
then going out
just
        as I drive beneath.

María Carmen's wheels
go around and around
to my music,
Kurt Cobain singing
"Lake of Fire."
Unplugged Nirvana.
And Lawson's laughing,
"What's this weird shit you listen to?"
*"Says the guy who listens to a group
called Bone Thugs-N-Harmony."*
"Says the dude who listens to a band
called Smashing Pumpkins."
And we both laugh
'cause music tastes don't matter
when you're brothers.

What does matter?

        Is what happens next.

red and blue

lights flash

reflecting on my dashboard

shining in my rearview

and I think

      This is it.

on the side of the road

I sit in the driver's seat,
hands on the wheel,
sweating,
shivering
so hard
I'm vibrating,
whispering to Lawson,
"*Please tell me you aren't carrying.*"

I look at Lawson.
His face gone pale.
He says,
"Shut up.
And be cool."

"*I can't,*"
I say.
"*I can't stop shaking.*"

"Be.
Cool,"
he says again,
"Anything happens,
you don't know shit.
No matter what. You say you don't know nothin'.

I got you."

a flashlight flashes

in my face
going from me
to Lawson,
then back to me.

A second officer stands outside Lawson's window,
another flashlight
scanning my best friend
up and down.

My officer says,
"ID and proof of insurance?"

I get out my wallet,
reach for my insurance card
in the glovebox
slow.
Then hand over both.

He studies them for a long time,
flashes the light in my eyes.
"You been drinking?"
"No, sir."
"What are you doing out this late?"
"*We just saw a movie*," I lie.
"We're heading home now."

"Uh-huh," he says.
"We'll be back."
The cops turn,
walking back to their car.

"what the fuck?"

I'm shaking,
trying
to catch
my breath,
waiting
waiting
waiting

for the cops to come back
pull out handcuffs
and arrest me.

"Be cool," Lawson says again.

"*Fuck you*,"
I hiss.

Then the cop starts walking back
and I bite my tongue
to keep

from screaming.

a bead of sweat

drips
down my forehead,
betraying me.

I wipe it away
just as the cop returns,
his friend on the other side.

The first cop says,
"Get out of the car."

"We didn't do nothin'," Lawson snaps.

The cop glares at Lawson.
"We didn't," Lawson says.
I glare at him,
my eyes telling him
to
shut
the fuck
up.

"Just you," the cop says to me.
"Come with me."

"*What'd I do?*" I ask.

He asks,
"Do I need to repeat myself?"

shoved

to the ground
a knee pressed into my back
handcuffs locking,
biting down
on my wrists
like a vicious wolf's
sharp and terrible teeth.

"You're under arrest,"
the cop is saying.
"You have the right to remain silent . . ."

Except I'm not silent
as I start to beg
and plead
that it wasn't me
that I'm innocent
even though
I'm not.

I'm complicit.

I shoulda said
           no.

(At least,
that's what I imagine
is gonna happen
any second
now.)

i follow the cop
who leads me
to the back of my car.

He points,
saying,

"Your taillight's out."

i think i'm safe
and oxygen
rushes back
into my burning lungs
'cause I didn't realize
I was holding my breath
'til now
'til
the law
shines his flashlight
in my face
asking,
"What's wrong?"

I'm this close
to pissing myself
for the first time
since second grade.

"*Nothin'*,"
I say,
"*nothin's wrong.*"

The cop asks,
"Then why are you sweating?"

Both police stare at me,
narrowed eyes,
suspicious as hell,
and my heart
wants to explode
bursting
from my chest.

And he says
what I feared he would say:

"Hands behind your head."

"turn around,"

he says,
and I obey.
Both his hands
pat
my shoulders
my armpits
my rib cage
my waist
my thighs
my knees
my ankles.
His fingers
and palms
searching
scanning
feeling
for anything
that proves
that I'm hiding

       something.

"this one's clean,"

the first cop says.

Then,
adds,

"Check the other one."

"get out of the car,"
the second cop says to Lawson.

Then,
"Hands behind your head.
Turn around."

"We didn't do nothin',"
Lawson says again.

The cop doesn't listen.
Both his hands
pat
Lawson's shoulders
Lawson's armpits
Lawson's rib cage
Lawson's waist
Lawson's thighs
Lawson's knees
Lawson's ankles.
The cop's fingers
and palms
searching
scanning
feeling
for anything
that proves
that Lawson is hiding
                    something

                              which he is. . . .

"this one's clean too,"

his cop says.

Relief
washes through me
my muscles going limp
'til

the first cop says,

"Watch them.

I'll search the car."

i am praying

Lawson didn't stash his drugs in my car
or it's over for me.

I'll go down with him.
I won't finish high school.
'cause I'll be in jail
and if I ever get out
I'll have a record
which means
no good jobs
which means
I won't be able
to pay my bills
which means

my life is over

      before it even started.

my eyes lock

on Lawson
who stares back
his hands behind his head
like
my hands behind my head
as one cop watches us
his hand
at his hip
on his gun
while
the other
searches my car.

Lawson's bright blue eyes
betray nothin'
while my brow
beads with more sweat.

My throat scolded by acid,
'til I swallow it down.

My legs shake with no control,
as if they aren't mine.

My lungs burn like fire
'cause I can't breathe.

My heart races,
pounding
so loud
I worry
the cops will hear it.

I am on the verge
of confessing
        everything

and pointing my finger
straight at Lawson

which is when

the second cops says,

"All clear."

the two cops

look us over
again
not sure
at all
what to make
of two boys
playing
at being
men
trying to be tough
but being
scared

      shitless.

Finally
the first cop says,

      "Go straight home."

sickness

washes through me
with hot, hot heat
like I might hurl,
puke all over myself,
as I get back in the car.

The cops get back in theirs,
and drive past us,

and away.

Lawson lets out this long
heavy sigh
that turns into a chuckle,
saying,
"That was fucking crazy, dude!"

"No. That was us almost getting arrested."

"They drove off. We're fine."

"Where are your drugs?"

Lawson smiles.
He pats his crotch.
"Secure in my briefs. Just behind the balls."

"Fuck,"
I say.
"Fuck fuck fuck fuck."

"Calm down,"
Lawson says.
"I told you, anything happens, it's on me.
You're safe.
I'd never let you take the fall."

"You say that,
but, Lawson, come on,
I'm guilty by association.

I can't jeopardize everything,
my whole future,
not for you,
not for this."

"What you saying?"

"I'm done.
I'm really, really done.
I can't do this anymore."

"You said that before."

"This time I mean it."

He says,
"Yeah, right."

on lawson's couch

I can't sleep.
I wanna go home.
But it's too late.
Mom knows I'm crashing over here tonight.
If I go home,
she'll ask why.
And I'm afraid,
if she asks,
I'll break down
fall down
to the ground
on my knees
in tears
and tell her
          everything.

          And what good would that do?

          Lawson is still my brother.

I gotta find
          some way
                    to help him
                              and make
                                        all of this

                                        stop.

APRIL

when i get home from work

Mom is sitting
at the kitchen table
her foot
tap
tap
tapping
against the linoleum floor.

I ask, worried,
"*What is it?*"

She touches an envelope
lying on the table.
She says,
"It's from a college."

I pick up the letter.
It feels too light
to contain
all the contents
of my future.

The letter,
light as a feather,
will tell me
if I will stay in the nest

or fly away.

i tear it open
but stop.
Not yet.

I breathe in.
I breathe out.

I look at Mom,
eyes eager,
almost trembling.

"No matter what happens,"
she says,
"I love you."

"I know."

I pull out the piece of paper

holding my fate

and unfold it.

"congratulations,"
it starts,
and then
I'm hopping
up and down
and then
so is Mom.

My future,

　　　　it's happening.

this paper

I hold in my hand
I can't put down
as if it might disappear
with my future in its sentences.

I hold it
gripping it
wondering how something so fragile
capable of being torn or burned
can have such powerful words
that make me vibrate
with joy
and reassurance
that all my hard work
has been worth it.

An hour later,
I sit in bed,
reading
and rereading
the piece of paper again and again
as if I might wake up from a dream

'til
my phone rings.

"i need a ride,"
Lawson says
through the phone.

I say,
"*I'm coming over.*
We gotta talk."

i've walked

across this street,
from my house
to Lawson's house
a thousand times
if not ten thousand times
in the last ten years

but this time

this time

      it feels farther.

"*i got accepted,*"
I say,
"*into college.*"

And Lawson,
his arms wrapping around me,
says,
"Fuck yeah."

He holds my face in his hands,
slaps one cheek gently,
saying,
"I'm so proud of you, brother."

Proud,
smiling,
the way a father would
if mine were still around.

"It's no surprise,"
Lawson says.
"I always knew you'd make it."

He pulls a joint
outta his pocket
and says,
"Mind if I celebrate?"

A knot expands in my throat,
knowing what I need to say

which is why

I can't.

I can't say it.

That look
of joy
for me

on Lawson's face,
I can't take it away.

        Not yet.

"you cool to gimme that ride?"

he asks.

"*I can't,*" I lie,
"*I gotta work.*"

alone

I drive out
to the edge of town
to the old lake
that's dried up
and gone.
I lie
on the hood
of María Carmen
staring up
at stars
in the sky
winking back at me.
Twinkle
       twinkle
           little star.

And I wish
that wishes were real
so I could wish
Lawson's life
would be better.

So I could wish
that somehow
I would fix this
make things right
and save Lawson
from himself

and from the world
that made him
into
      this.

But wishes aren't real

and I have no idea

how to help

my brother

my best friend

my other half.

i make a promise
not to others
but
      to myself

I promise
under the moon
that
      I am done.

No more rides
for Lawson.
No more rides
for me.
For my tomorrow.
For all my tomorrows.

I don't wanna lose my friend.
But I gotta make a choice.

It's him or me.

And right now

        it has to be

            me.

on monday
I get up early
and drive to school

without Lawson.

when i see lawson
in the hallway
I duck and turn into the next hallway.
I know
I'm a coward.

But how do I say
"I'm done with this,"
when I've said it
so many times before
and didn't stick to it?

How do I say
"I'm done with this,
and I mean it this time,"
and still look him in the eyes
when they are filled with so much hurt

already.

there's no more running

when Lawson sits down next to me,
at lunch,
asking,
"What the fuck?
You ditched me this morning.
I had to ride the fucking bus."

Like a Band-Aid
over a scabbed wound,
I rip it off,
saying,
"*I can't, Lawson.
I can't risk it anymore.*"

"Risk what?"
"*Everything.*"
I say,
"*I can't drive you if you're holding.*"

"If you don't know—"
"*But I do know,*" I say.
"*I always know
'cause you're always holding.
And I can't.
I'm sorry.*"

"You're sorry?"
Lawson sneers.
"You're sorry?
You can't drop me like this.
We had a deal."

"*I'll still help you study.
I want you to graduate.*"

"Fuck that,"
he snaps. "You're supposed to be there for me.
Through thick and thin.
You're my brother."

"I still am.
Always will be.
But I can't help you.
Not if you're carrying."

"What am I supposed to do?!
You know my deal.
I gotta support myself.
My mom.
I gotta do this if I want a roof over my head,
if I wanna feed myself."

"I know.
But you gotta stop selling before you ruin your life."

"My life is already ruined!"
he screams.

He slams his fist against the table.

"You know what?
I'm sick of this shit," Lawson snaps,
"this tug-of-war bullshit you do.
One minute you can drive me.
The next you can't.
Fuck all that.
We brothers or not?"

"We are."

"Then you gotta be there for me."

"I am,
but not if you're selling."

Lawson slaps my lunch tray,
it flies across the table,
off the edge,
slapping the floor loud
with a clatter and clack

so everyone is staring at us
at our family drama
again.

"Fuck that noise,"
Lawson shouts.
"And fuck you."

He gets up
and storms away
like a hurricane
ready to destroy
everything in his path

even himself.

after school

I sit in my car,
wrestling with myself,
waiting for Lawson,
wanting to offer him a ride home,
even though I know
I can't.

When I see him
walk into the parking lot
and offer up his magic handshake
to one student
after the next,
I know I'm doing
the right thing

                by driving away

                        without him.

monday

leads to Tuesday

leads to Wednesday

leads to Thursday

leads to Friday

leads to Saturday

leads to Sunday

leads to Monday

      again,

and still

Lawson won't talk to me.

But

    I haven't talked to him

          either.

i keep busy
with school
homework
work-work
and more homework
studying
for this test
and that test
prepping for finals
trying to occupy my mind
with definitions and equations and dates
so I don't have to think
about Lawson.

when i come home from work
I pull into my driveway,
reeking of wasted food
and industrial-strength dishwashing soap
and a paper paycheck in my pocket
that pays me the bare minimum
of legal wages.

I roll up my windows,
hop outta the car
lock it
about to go inside
when I look over my shoulder
across the street
at Lawson's.

The streetlight is out,
the porch lights are off,
as if shadow has swallowed
him and his home
like a lighthouse
that doesn't work
leaving Lawson
lost
in the shadows
of darkest night
among the raging black waters
ready to dash his body
against the rocks
'til
he disappears
beneath the surface.

"i've noticed,"

Mom starts,
"that you don't hang out
with Lawson
anymore."

I sit there
at the table
chewing dinner
(tacos
made by Mom)
in silence
except the crunch
of the crunchy shells.

"You wanna talk about it?"

"I really don't."

"I know it's hard,"
Mom says,
"but you're doing the right thing.
Lawson doesn't deserve
a friend like you."

"He's not my friend,"
I bark,
*"he's my brother.
Other than you,
he's the only family I got."*

I stomp to my room

and slam the door

hard

and on purpose.

at lunch
I sit
by myself
eating
missing Lawson's
jokes
charms
presence
and laughter
across from me
in the school cafeteria
where most students
have someone
to sit with.

"what are you reading?"

When I look up
it isn't Lawson.

It's Vanessa.

"The Awakening. By Kate Chopin. It's about this woman—"

"—who bucks the societal norms of being a wife and a mother at the
turn of the nineteenth century when she falls in love with a man who is
not her husband.
I read it.
Have you gotten to the ending?"

"Not yet."

"I hope you like it."
Vanessa smiles,
adding,
"Come sit with us."

lawson is dealing

across the street
outta his house.

I know this
'cause Mom knows this
peeking outta our window
watching
as strange people
enter his house
and leave shortly (too quickly) after.

"He's bringing down the neighborhood
selling that trash,"
she says.
"I should call the cops."

"*Don't*," I growl.

"Diego—"

"*Don't*,"
I say,
"*or I'll never speak to you again.*"

I hate Mom for making me say that.
I hate Lawson for making me say that, too.

Now
I am angry
at the two people I love most
when all I want
is everyone
to be happy

and be safe

and be by my side

        forever.

later

after Mom has gone to bed
without another word
to me
I walk to our front window
peeking between plastic blinds
to watch

Lawson sitting on his porch
drumming a foot
'til a white SUV pulls up.
He struts over
sneaks a glance both ways
before sticking his head
and hand
into the window.

It's an exchange.

Only there's no magic
in the way he moves.
He's not trying to hide what he does
not anymore
as if
he wants to get caught
by becoming a drive-thru window
though not offering up
burgers and fries and shakes
but instead
weed and blow and pills.

My mind races
to imagine

cops rolling up
red and blue flashing
wrestling him to the ground
handcuffing him
before taking him away.

Or,
a deal gone wrong
his customers
pulling a gun
pulling the trigger
pop pop pop
shooting him dead
in the street
where we used to play.

I don't know which is worse.

A life ruined

or a life ended

or if there's any difference
                            at all.

when i hear it

at the other end
of the crowded school hallway
I already know
it's Lawson
shouting.

I dodge students,
making my way
to the deep timbre of his voice,
and find him
yelling at Lori.

Holding a piece of paper
in her face
Lawson screaming,
"You dump me in a fucking note?!"

Her voice cracks,
fear filling her eyes.
"Lawson, stop. Please.
People are looking."

"I don't give a fuck.
Tell me why."

Tears stream down her face.
"I love you. I do.
But I can't."

"Why?!"

Lori takes a look
at the gathering crowd
and whispers,
"You know why."

Lawson sneers.
"So you just abandon me.
Think you're better than me."

"No, I don't.
You know I don't.
I just . . .
I can't right now.
I need to focus on my future.
On college and stuff."

"You sound just like him."

"Who?"

"Benny."

Lawson's face is
gritted teeth
crimson cheeks
dilated pupils.

His fists clench.
He punches a locker

as Mr. Salazar pushes through the crowd,
shouting, "What's going on?"

Seeing Lawson's rage
a familiar volcano
about to blow,
I step between
my friend
and my teacher,
my arms raised, fingers wide to each
to calm their aggressions,
saying,
"*Everything's cool.*"

"No," Lawson growls.
"Everything is not cool.
You. Lori. This whole school.
This whole life.
It's fucked.

It's all fucked!"

"*Lawson—*"
I start.

That's when he turns

        and punches me

he hits me in the face
so hard

I fall back

onto the floor

dazed

the blood

comes out fast

pouring

gushing

outta my nose

as I look up
                      at Lawson

his eyes

waver
with regret
and confusion
at what he's done
as if his fists betrayed him

his eyes
glisten
wet
afraid

                    and there he is

I see him
for the first time
in years
my brother
          is really
                    a scared little boy

locked inside
the shell of a man
too old before his time.

Our eyes lock
for the briefest of moments

before he screams
this deep
guttural
animal
wail

that pummels my heart
harder
than any fist
ever could.

Seeing he has an audience,
Lawson tries to take off . . .

"not another step,"

Principal Villalobos commands.
"My office. Now."

The hall is filled with silence
despite hundreds of teens
and dozens of teachers
watching
a showdown
between student
and authority.

Lawson's body,
a mountain
of fury,
is ready to challenge
anyone in his way.
And the principal is in his.

"Why? So you can tell me what a failure I am?
What a piece of shit I am?
That my life is worth nothin'?"
Lawson growls,
a shaking in his voice only I can hear.
"Fuck that.
I'm done.
I'm out."

He thunders toward the exit
a storm, not on the horizon
but here, in a school hallway.

"You walk out that door,"
the principal calls,
"you won't be permitted back in this school.
You won't graduate."

Lawson,
his back to all of us,
says,

"I was never gonna graduate.

I never had a chance."

MAY

like the wheels

on María Carmen,
days spin by,
rolling ever forward
though never in reverse,
hurling me
toward graduation
like a comet
ready to hit the planet
and destroy the past.
I will go off to college,
this town left behind me,
and all I will take
are memories
including those
of a friendship
now gone.

Lawson
being replaced
by a diploma?

It hardly seems

      like a fair trade.

without lawson

the school feels empty
the hallways less alive
the cafeteria less joyous

even when
I'm surrounded by people
new friends
at a new lunch table

my heart aches

incomplete

part of it stolen away

by the neighbor

    who became my best friend

      who became my brother.

sitting next to

Vanessa and Lori and Johnson
at lunch,
we talk about life
after graduation,
a topic
I always avoided
with Lawson,
not wanting him to feel
apart
from me.

But now
my laughter
is warm and optimistic
and at the same time
a betrayal
'cause I wouldn't know these people
if Lawson hadn't introduced me
and pushed me
from inside my turtle's shell
out
into the world
so that I could experience it
to the fullest.

every day

is a reminder
of Lawson.

When I leave my house
(I see his house)
when I come home
(I see his home)
and I can't help
but gaze
across the street
at something missing
here with me.

Even when my phone rings
I expect his voice
on the other end
saying, "I need a ride."

But usually,
the call is just work
or Mom's sponsor.

I'm glad she has help.
I do.

But I'd rather the call
be from Lawson.

hands on hips

frustrated,
Mom asks,
"Why didn't you order
graduation invitations?"

"And send them to who?
The only people I want there,
the only family I have
is you and . . . "

I can't even say his name

      without

            a violent sting

                  in my chest

                      and deeper

                          in my soul.

lawson laughs

as he falls back on my bed
holding his sides
as if his guts will spill out
onto the sheets
from laughing so hard.

At least
that's what I imagine
as my reflection
stares back at me
from a mirror
wearing
a black cap
and gown
making me look
like some old judge
or academic
from a century
way in the past.

Lawson
in my head
still laughing
says,
"You look like a church choir singer.
I wouldn't wear that shit if you paid me,"
which makes me smile
'til he adds,

"and now I never will."

graduation

arrives too quick
then moves too slow
after Lori
our salutatorian
has given her speech
and they call our names
one by one by one
'til
they call my name
one of my names
        not Benny,
but

"Diego Miguel Benevides"

and I walk across the stage
Mom shouting
her heart out
from an audience
full of proud packs
of parents
and families
and friends
while I only have
her.

All
year
a swell
of anticipation
grew in my lungs
ready for this moment
to stop looking at the future
as an alien
and see

                tomorrow

                        as today.

i can't help but smile
shaking hands
with the principal
who smiles
as she places a blue and gold padded diploma jacket
in my hands.

Instructed
by some inner instinct,
I hold it up
for all the world
to see
        that I did it.

                Me.

                        I really did it.

Walking back to my folding chair,
I glance
to the far end of the auditorium
by the exit door
and see
a familiar figure
standing there.
Lawson.

He nods
with the most subtle
of proud smiles
and then
                    he's gone.

It's so brief.

I wonder

                      if I imagined it.

back in my seat

among fidgeting peers
I grip the diploma case
Principal Villalobos handed me on stage,
gleaming gold and cobalt
on plastic
imitating leather.
My delight
of achievement
flickers
quivers
trembles

as I open it,

           and it is empty.

I recall
someone said
they would mail us
the real diploma
stickered and embossed
later
'cause they don't want us
these overwhelmed graduates
to lose it
in all the goings-on
of a busy ceremony
filled with laughter and tears
among parents,
grandparents,
cousins,
friends,
and so on.

But still
      I feel cheated
                for me
      but also
                for my mom
                who deserves

to hold the real thing
since she deserves
as much credit
as I do.

after square hats fly
and fall to the earth,
the student body
scatters
into packs
while I only have one
person to go to.

Mom
won't let go
showering kisses
on my forehead
and cheeks
and ears,
saying
over and over again,
"I am so proud of you."

I love her.
More than anyone.
It is good to have her here.

But
still
I wish
Lawson
who I also love
was here
in his own cap and gown
cheering
beside me
for all of
                    his
                            tomorrows
                            that are yet to come.

"how should we celebrate?"

Mom asks.
"*Dinner,*"
I say,
"*you and me.*
Then
I'm going to a party
with Vanessa and Lori."

Her brow creases,
eye lids narrowing
with concern.

"*I deserve this,*"
I say.
"*It's been a long year.*
And I won't be drinking.
I'm the designated driver.
I just wanna go
and have some fun."

"You're right,"
Mom says.
"You deserve it."
She adds
as I walk out the door,
"Be safe."

I kiss her on the forehead,
saying,
            "*I will be.*"

i think
it's strange
being at a party
and actually
feeling comfortable
in my own skin
drinking ginger ale
from a Solo cup
dancing with Vanessa
to bumping music
laughing as she whispers
words tickling my ear
tingling my whole body with heat
which makes me
just another teenager
living his life.

It's stranger
being at a party
and enjoying myself
like all the stress
of high school
has melted away
revealing a new me
beneath.

But what's strangest

      is being at a party

           without Lawson.

that's when i see him

Lawson
a magician again
only . . .
instead
of his fingers transforming
green bagged bud
into
green cash money,
his handshake with others
is just that . . .

      a handshake.

The only magic he's using
       is making people smile
           with his natural charm.

When he sees me

he makes his way over

"can i talk to you?"
he asks me.

we sit outside
on the back porch
watching seniors talking
watching seniors dancing
watching seniors drinking
watching seniors laughing
watching seniors
jumping
      into Johnson's pool
           with abandon

to baptize themselves
with a fresh start
and start writing
a new chapter
in their lives.

Lawson though?

He is quiet a long time,
smoking his menthol
before I finally speak.

"was that you?"

I ask.
"Today? At graduation?"

Lawson inhales,
lungs full of smoke,
saying,
"I wouldn't let you
graduate
without me being there."

He exhales,
the smoke
uncurling midair
fading into dark midnight sky
pinpricked by light
from galaxies
millions of light-years away
traveling here
to watch
us
living.

Twinkle
        twinkle
                little star.

Me wondering
if Lawson could make a wish
what it would be

        as we drift

                into silence.

"last night i had this dream,"

Lawson finally says.

"I was driving a truck,
one of them old rusty Fords,
like from the nineteen fifties or somethin',
riding
down this dusty dirt road
middle of this big green field
of tall stalks,
crops and stuff,
not pot,
but like food
like corn or wheat or somethin'.
I parked,
next thing I know,
I'm farming.
Digging in the ground,
spreading seeds,
watering plants,
cutting 'em down,
picking produce,
making this big harvest.
I got all this dirt
under my fingernails,
my hands are old,
wrinkled and shit,
I mean not ancient or nothin',
but they look all rough
'cause I'm like forty years old.
Anyways
I take this basket
all full up
of fruits and vegetables
my dog following
(you know I always wanted a dog)
and I go inside
this old house,
paint peeling outside

which I keep meaning to fix
but it's mine,
the house, I mean.
Inside,
I got this wife,
kinda plain, but pretty too,
making a pie
from scratch.
I kiss her on the cheek,
then start washing
the fruits and vegetables
'cause I plan to make dinner.
Me, cooking? Like, yeah right.
But these two kids
run into the kitchen
boy and girl
like five and seven,
chasing the dog
them laughing, dog's tail wagging,
and I'm all 'Slow down!'
rolling my eyes at my wife,
who laughs,
not at me,
but with me,
and this
      big
         stupid
           grin
              is all over my face.

Then I woke up.

      I woke up

        and I was crying.

Like
sobbing.

But I'm not sure
if it was 'cause
I was happy from the dream

or just so sad
        to come back
                to this life."

lawson takes another drag

from his cig
blows out smoke
and looks over at me.

"Sounds like Candide.
That book by Voltaire."

"Thought you said
that guy's life started good
and got worse and worse."

"It did.
But in the end,
he and his friends
ended up on a farm
cultivating their garden.
It was kinda nice."

"So it had a happy ending?"

"Depends on how you look at it.

                    But I'd like to think so."

"i miss you, broseph,"

Lawson says.
"Feels weird not talking to you every day."

*"I know.
I missed you too."*

Lawson takes another drag
from his cigarette,
then puts it out,
twisting it into the ground
'til the spark of flame
goes out
ashes to ashes.

"I shouldn't'a done all those things.
Hitting you.
Putting you in a bad position.
Making you give me rides when I was holding.
I really fucked up.
I'm sorry.
For everything."

I wanna say
It's okay.
But it's not.
So I don't' say nothin'.

We sit for a while
watching our peers
swimming and drinking and laughing

carefree.

Lawson asks,
"We good?"

I answer,
"Yeah, we're good."

We
(real quick)
bump fists,
shake hands,
bump shoulders.

"would it be okay,"

Lawson asks,
"if you gave me a ride home?"

"*Lawson—*"
I start.

He puts both hands up
in surrender,
"I ain't holding.
I took the night off.
You can check my pockets.
I wanted to just be here
just another kid
one last time
before all of ya
move on."

I hesitate.

Then
I nod.
"Yeah,
Yeah, I'll give you a ride . . . "

one hand out the window

trying to catch the wind
my other hand
on the steering wheel.
Breeze rolls in
tossing my hair
this way and that.

Lawson turns up the radio
belting out
"If I ruled the world
Still livin' for today, in these last days and times,"
knowing every word by heart,
of Nas's "If I Ruled the World"
while I know
just the chorus
the part featuring
Lauryn Hill.

But Vanessa and Lori
know all the words too
singing from the backseat.

Outside of her house,
Lori hugs Lawson
after their long talk,
him apologizing to her too,
and Vanessa kisses me
all too briefly
on the lips.

Then it's just me and Lawson.

"wanna come inside?"

Lawson asks.

"Play a round of Mario Kart?"

*"If you want me to kick your ass,
sure."*

"You kidding?
I always win."

"Since when?"

And it's just like
old times.
Like
we're kids again.

that's when
Trent
and two friends
kick in the door

guns out.

i'm waiting to die
the second
they kick in the door
—the drug dealer
and his crew—
'cause I know
it's gonna be bad
'cause their
guns
are already out.

I'm shoved up against the wall,
punched in the stomach
so hard
I
          can't
                    breathe.

A tattooed forearm
crushes my throat,
choking me.

Then
the gun
          the gun
                    the *GUN*
pinches my temple,
metal pressing into skin
as I stare cross-eyed
at the finger on the trigger,
waiting
for my brains to smear the wall
like red paint . . .

That's when
Lawson's dealer
starts screaming,
"WHERE'S MY MONEY?!"

i can't breathe
thinking
this is how i die
this is how i die
this is how i die

lawson's eyes

meet mine
apologizing
again and again
and again

one gun
aimed at my head
by the tattooed giant
pinning me against the wall.

The other gun
in Trent's hand
aimed at Lawson.

The third guy
looking out the window
is paranoid
and tweaked out.

"where's my fucking money?!"

Trent is screaming,
waving his gun
at Lawson.

Lawson has his hands up
empty
in surrender
saying,
"Trent, man,
I need more time."

"That's what you said last week
and the week before
and the week before that.
I ain't playing any more games."

"I ain't playing games,
I swear,"
Lawson says
as calm as he can.
"I told you,
I can't move it that fast."

"Fucking excuses,"
Trent roars.

"I can give it back,"
Lawson pleads.
"I can give you the money
for what I sold
and give you the rest of the drugs.
I have it all.
Not a cent missing.
Not a pill missing."

"That's not how this works,"
Trent says.
"I supply.
You sell.

And you're not holding up your end of the bargain.
I guess
         I need to teach you a lesson."

"so what do i do?"
Trent asks.
"Shoot you,

or,"

he looks at me,

"shoot your friend?"

**as
quick
as
a
bullet**
Lawson
rushes
Trent
tackles
him
to
the
ground
punches
him
in
the
face.

as
quick
as
a
bullet

the
tattooed
giant
lets
me
go
and
points
his
gun
at
Lawson.

as
quick

as
a
bullet

I
shove
past
the
giant
and
jump
toward
my
brother

as
quick
as
a
bullet

a
gun
goes
off
with
a

BANG

time slows down

as Lawson

and I

stare at one another.

His blue eyes

blond stubble

face pale

gold chains around his neck

his white shirt

now stained

with flecks

of

red

I don't wanna lose Lawson

not like this.

But

that's

that's when

I realize

it's not lawson's blood.

it's mine.

"fuck,"

Trent says,
"fuck fuck fuck fuck,"
staring at me.
My fingers caress
the new window
peeking
inside my chest
as if these hands
can keep the wind out
and the blood in
as my knees buckle
and I crumble
to the ground.

"Fuck,"
Trent says,
"fuck fuck fuck fuck.
We gotta go.
We gotta go now.
Let's get the fuck outta here."

Trent
and his crew
fly fast
fleeing
leaving the door
wide open
so I can see
my own house
across the street.

"no no no no no no,"
Lawson says,
on his knees
pressing his hands
over the hole
in my chest.

there's so much blood

Lawson's hands
are soaked in it
as I
leak out
of my own body

"stay with me, brother,"

Lawson cries,
"stay with me, Benny.
You're gonna be okay.
You're gonna be okay."

Eyes fluttering
struggling to stay open
I shake my head softly.
"I
don't
think
I
am."

"No no no no,"
Lawson says,
"please no,
God please."
Pushing his palms
against me
harder
trying to hold me in
as I flow out
between his fingers
like water.

"Why did you do that?"
he moans.
"Why did you take that bullet for me?"

"It's okay,"
I say
as it gets harder to think,
"you would
have done
the same
for
me."

"It shoulda been me, Benny.
Why didn't you let him shoot me?"

"'Cause you're
my friend.
My ride-
or-die.
My brother."

"Don't do this,"
Lawson pleads,
wet streaming down
his cheeks
onto his
lips,
saying,
"Don't die, Benny."
Don't die."

"Make me
a promise,"
I whisper,
feeling
farther
and
farther
away
from
my
own
body.

"Promise me,

you'll
do

better.
You'll

be

better.

Get

out

of

this

town

and

            just

                    be

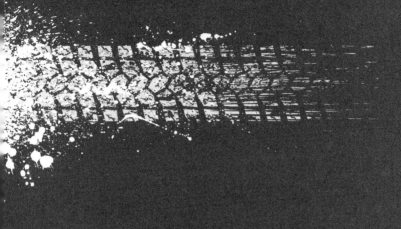

LAWSON

i'm driving
alone
out into nowhere
'cause that's what I shoulda done
a long time ago
before

what happened to Benny

happened.

World never had my back.
But Benny did.

And
he paid for it
bought it
with his life
even though
I wasn't selling.

Benny.
Diego Miguel Benevides.
My brother.

Out here
middle of nothin' Texas
riding west
ain't a goddamn thing
in any direction
except
rocks
and sand
caught in the wind
like baby tornadoes
and actual, whatdya call 'em,
tumbleweeds
like in 'em Saturday mornin' cartoons

Benny made me watch
when we was little

all under this big light blue sky
sun shining all bright
and happy
like no one dies
every
single
day
even though they do.

World keeps moving
wind keeps blowing
tires keep rolling
and I keep driving
toward

I dunno.

Not sure where
I'm going
but sure as shit know
I couldn't stay in that town.
Not another fuckin' day.
Not with Trent there.
Not with Benny's mom across the street.
Not with everything
everywhere
in that place
reminding me
of my friend
and all the dumb shit
I did.

Now
got a duffel bag
one of 'em gas stop sandwiches
bag of chips and coke
(the soda, not the drug)

and a shoe box
filled with enough cash
to start over
somewhere.

Maybe

I dunno

maybe

that dream I had
that one time
with the farm
and the wife
and the kids
and the dog
maybe
maybe that'll happen

and maybe

maybe

(I hope)

I'll finally
make Benny proud
the way
I
was
always
proud of him.

my appreciations

To the past . . . It wasn't an easy ride. All my firsts came too early: violence, alcohol, drugs, losing friends along the way. But other firsts came right on time: books, comics, reading, learning that (if I put in the work) the written word was something I might sway—when everything else in my life was out of control. So I taught myself to put my pain on paper in poetry. The hurt was still there, but it was somehow lessened by sharing my secrets with a spiral notebook—until four assholes ripped it from my hands, read my words out loud, called me a fag for writing "shitty girl poetry," and tore pages out and in half, then tossed them in the trash. Like I said, not an easy ride. But now, looking back, I know I wouldn't be *here* if I hadn't been *there.*

To the present . . . After decades of research, Thich Nhat Hanh books, diet changes, exercise, therapy, antidepressants, yoga, self-help books, and finally giving up on being happy—I kinda found happiness. I'm in a good spot, but boy oh boy was it hard to get here. But I couldn't have done it without help. Friends: Kim Hulse, Katie Kubert, Joe Gallagher, RJ Williams, William Heus, and Ryan Perella. Family: Shelby Tieken and Amber Lucas, my aunt Lora, and of course, my abuela, Catalina Caldwell. My husband and partner, Mark Sikes, I don't know how you put up with me. My dog, Toby, I will always give you rubs. And of course book folks: Brent Taylor, who found me and gave me a chance. Simon Boughton, who found me and took a risk. Cathy Berner, who always has my back (and makes me smile every time a One Direction alum comes on the radio).

And to the future . . . I'm finally living my dream, writing books full-time . . . never realizing (until now) that being an author means being a friend to readers and educators and librarians and booksellers. And that? That makes me feel like the luckiest sonovawitch this side of Abilene. I don't know how I made it from Texas trailer trash to an actual gosh-darn writer, but I'm grateful—so grateful—more grateful than I can put into words—and I plan to spend every day for the rest of my life being grateful that I get to turn my ideas and thoughts and feelings into something meaningful found in sentences printed on pages inside of books.

Thank you to every single person who holds this book in their hands. I'm sending you psychic hugs.* But if we meet in person—or *when* we meet in person—make sure to ask for a hug. I give great hugs. Hugs rule.

(*That includes you Arthur, and your new brother, Teddy, who was born [no joke] about five minutes ago. Your dad just texted me pictures of y'all and I can't stop crying the happiest of tears. You are the future, and I can't wait to see what you do.)

And please, every one of you, remember: life isn't an easy ride for any of us. But it sure is worth it. Keep driving.

Big hugs,
Rex Ogle
May 2024